Trouble at

Featherlow Forbes Menswear

PATRINA McKENNA

Publisher: Patrina McKenna

patrina.mckenna@outlook.com

ISBN-13: 978-1-8381827-0-0

Also by Patrina McKenna

Romantic comedy with a twist!

Truelove Hills
Truelove Hills – Mystery at Pebble Cove
Truelove Hills – The Matchmaker
Granny Prue's Bucket List
Christmas with the Neighbours
Trouble at Featherlow Forbes Menswear

Feel good fantasy for all the family!

GIANT Gemstones
A Galaxy of Gemstones
The Gemstone Dynasty
Enrico's Journey
Summer Camp at Tadgers Blaney Manor

DEDICATION

For my family and friends

1

CONFERENCE PREPARATIONS

September was always a busy month at Featherlow Forbes Menswear; it was the time of year the company held its annual conference. With the Global Top 100 members of the organisation descending on the Head Office in London, Amelie and Fifi were rushed off their feet.

'Amelie! Are the name badges ready? They need to be with Fifi on reception before lunch. The driver's booked to take everything to the hotel at one o'clock. I'll head over with him to make sure everything's set up for tomorrow.'

Amelie smiled at Lord Featherlow's Executive Assistant. 'That's no problem, Grant. I've just finished the last-minute changes. I'll pop down to reception now.'

Carrying the box with the badges, Amelie waited for the lift. Grant rushed over to help her. 'Here, let me carry the box. It's the least I can do after all the work you've put in over the last two weeks. I can't believe it's this time of the year again. Are you going to the wine bar later? If so, I'll buy you a drink.'

Amelie's eyes twinkled as she took in Grant's dimpled smile, neatly-styled dark brown hair and hazel eyes. 'I hope you're not flirting with me Grant McGuire; you know very well I'm engaged.'

Grant sighed. 'You can't blame a guy for trying. Where is this fiancé of yours, anyway? You never bring him along to any work events. Don't tell me you're embarrassed by him. Is it a case of Beauty marrying the Beast?'

Amelie managed a laugh. 'Behave yourself! Brendan works unsociable hours as a personal trainer. He also treats his body as a temple. Drunken work do's aren't his scene.'

'Great that you're not bringing him along tomorrow night then! The Featherlow Forbes team certainly know how to party.'

'Don't remind me! I'm still recovering from last year. I'll be easy on the alcohol and hog roast this year. I have a wedding dress fitting on Saturday. My party days will soon be over.'

The lift door opened, and the couple stepped inside. Amelie pressed the "Ground Floor" button. The descent from the fourth floor took seconds. Grant carried the box to the reception desk. 'You're far too young to stop partying.'

Fifi stood up and widened her baby blue eyes. 'That's what I keep telling her. Twenty-eight is far too young to get married.' Fifi lowered her eyes and kept her real opinion to herself. Twenty-eight wasn't too young for Amelie to get married – if it was to someone other than Brendan.

Amelie's sandy hair was waist length and tied in plaits. She kept throwing them over her shoulders, and Grant caught one that skimmed inches from his face. 'Why do you always wear your hair in plaits? Have you ever thought of a pixie cut like Fifi?'

Fifi did a twirl to accentuate her short blonde hair, and Amelie suppressed a shudder. 'Brendan likes my plaits. It reminds him of when we met at school. He was my first boyfriend, you know.'

Grant and Fifi answered unanimously, 'We know.'

Amelie turned round and headed back towards the lift while Grant remained to speak to Fifi. 'We also know they've known each other for over twenty years. That's nearly a life sentence. Why's she so hooked on marrying him?'

'They're childhood friends. They went to school together and started dating when they were sixteen. It hasn't all been plain sailing though; Amelie broke up with Brendan the first Christmas they were together. It took ten years for them to rekindle things.'

'How long have they been together this time?'

'Two years. But Amelie has to pay a heavy price. It's due to Brendan that she doesn't like Christmas. He says he can never get over the fact that she dumped him at Christmas, and he's made her promise that they'll never celebrate it again. In Brendan's eyes, it's the worst time of the year.'

'Aren't they getting married on Christmas Eve?'

'Yep. There won't be a Christmas tree or Santa hat in sight. The venue has been warned. I'm sure it's so they have a good excuse this year to disappear ahead of any festive family gatherings.'

'That's a bit weird, don't you think?'

'Definitely.'

'A recipe for disaster if you ask me.'

'Don't I know it!'

'Well, what are we going to do about it?'

'I've been racking my brains, trust me. I've got some ideas.'

'Meet me in the wine bar after work. Two heads are better than one.'

*

Amelie checked her watch; it was six o'clock. All the plans were in place for tomorrow's conference. It was safe to make a quick getaway before she was wheeled off to the wine bar by Fifi or Grant. Checking her messages as she waited for the lift, Amelie wasn't surprised to see one from Brendan. She tutted; that man worked far too hard. He had another client this evening. Well, at least Amelie wouldn't have to pop into the supermarket on the way home to buy healthy ingredients for dinner. With Brendan sorting himself out, she could grab a microwavable ready meal and spend the evening ticking things off her wedding "to do" list.

Striding through the reception area and turning to wave to Fifi, Amelie bumped into "Action Man" who was dragging his suitcase behind him. 'Hi, Amelie! It should be a great conference this year. The wind's picking up out there. It'll soon be Christmas!'

Amelie smiled and headed for the revolving door. What did he say? Why did he mention Christmas? Amelie cringed when she thought back to last year.

She'd never forgive Grant for putting her on the spot. He devised an "ice breaker" for the conference and plucked six people from the audience to say three things about themselves, only two of which were true. Amelie blushed at the thought. All she could remember was being dragged onto the stage and muttering something like: 'I'm engaged to be married. I'm a good cook. I love Christmas.' Of course, they all thought she wasn't a good cook – that must be the untruth – no-one guessed she didn't like Christmas.

Action Man wasn't really called that. It was a name Fifi had invented after she found out he was head of the Canadian operation and liked skiing and white-water rafting. His real name was Chad Lagerfield. Amelie stopped in her tracks and stared at her reflection in a shop window. She took out her purse and unfolded an intricate drawing of a Christmas tree that had been slipped under her hotel room door during last year's conference. Surely the dashing Chad Lagerfield wasn't the artist? He was blonde, tanned, impeccably dressed, and didn't wear a wedding ring. Why did he smile at her so knowingly just now when he mentioned Christmas?

Amelie was abruptly brought back to reality. She had been staring into the window of Fifi's hairdressing salon. Amelie had waited inside for Fifi on many occasions; her friend regularly popped in for a quick trim after work. Giovanni stepped outside. 'Miss

Amelie! I knew you could not resist having a makeover before your wedding. Miss Fifi said I could work wonders on your hair. Come inside and let me turn you into a princess.'

With Fifi and Grant complaining about her plaits, and now Giovanni making it clear that her hair was a mess, Amelie stepped into the salon. The only nagging feeling she had was that Brendan might not like her new haircut. Still, it was only hair. At the end of the day, it would grow back. Sipping a cappuccino and watching her plaits fall to the floor, Amelie felt a sense of liberation. She was like a chrysalis turning into a butterfly. Brendan could not fail to be impressed.

2

THE WINE BAR PLOT

S everal members of the Featherlow Forbes team had descended on the wine bar, making it difficult for Grant and Fifi to speak in private. They found a small table in the corner of the room and huddled together. There were nods and winks in their direction, which they chose to ignore. Their colleagues could think what they liked; they were doing this for Amelie.

Fifi tucked into a packet of crisps, without offering one to Grant. The lengths she would go to for Amelie were unbelievable. Still, Fifi had a plan, and she was about to unveil it to her co-conspirator.

'I went to the gym at lunchtime.'

'Oh, I see, that's why you're starving now and not

offering me a crisp.'

Fifi screwed the empty packet up. 'That will be my last packet for quite some time. I've joined Brendan's twelve-week Boot Camp. It's called: Lose a Stone Before Christmas.'

'Surely you don't need to lose a stone?'

Fifi blushed and whispered. 'The little upstart told me I need to lose two!'

'Little? Is he little?'

'I'd say he's smaller than average height. Hairless all over and arms and legs wider than the pumpkins I'll be buying for Halloween.'

Grant pulled a face. 'Errrgh! No wonder Amelie doesn't want us to meet him. Does he know you work with her?'

'No! I didn't blow my cover. Hopefully, I'll only need to suffer for a couple of weeks before I find out he's offering more than exercise classes to one or more of his clients. That would be the best result. Amelie would leave him straight away. Nothing better than a nice clean break.'

Grant rubbed his chin. 'But what if Amelie really loves him? What if our instincts are wrong?'

'Does she look like a lovestruck bride to you?'

Grant shook his head, and Fifi sighed. 'There's a dullness in those turquoise eyes. They should be sparkling. It annoys me that Amelie doesn't make the most of herself – she could be stunning.'

'I know what you mean; it's as if she's holding herself back. People can't see past those dreadful plaits.'

'Hi, Fifi. Grant. Mind if I join you? I've just checked in at the hotel and thought I'd find some of our colleagues in here.'

Grant pulled out a stool for Chad Lagerfield. 'I bumped into Amelie earlier. Is she not popping in for a drink?'

Fifi slid a glance at Grant. 'Oh, Amelie's busy tonight. She'll be at the hotel first thing in the morning though, ready for the conference. We're all staying over for the party tomorrow night too.'

Chad flashed a white smile. 'Ah, that's great! I find her intriguing. It's a shame she can't cook. Let's hope her future husband is good in the kitchen.'

Fifi burst into giggles. 'Amelie's an excellent cook. She's also engaged at the moment. The thing that wasn't true about her is that she loves Christmas. Amelie has taken a dislike to the holiday season.'

Chad frowned. 'How strange. Is there any way we

can change her stance on that? Christmas is the best time of the year.'

Fifi downed her wine, and Chad signalled to the waiter for another bottle. Fifi muttered, 'We've no chance in changing her mind about Christmas unless we get rid of Brendan.'

Grant kicked Fifi under the table, and Chad raised his eyebrows. 'Who's Brendan?'

Fifi sat up straight. 'Oh, just an old rabbit. It died at Christmas years ago.'

Chad gulped. 'She's still got the rabbit?'

Grant poured more wine for Chad. 'Only the ashes. It's no big deal. I hear you're making a presentation tomorrow. Have you sent me through your slides as a backup? It's best not to take any chances; we may have some IT blips.'

Chad reached into his pocket. 'Here's a memory stick. There's a copy of everything on there.'

Fifi checked her watch. 'Is that the time? I must get off. See you both in the morning.'

*

Amelie shook her head and watched as her new short-styled sandy hair fell back into place. 'You're a genius, Giovanni!'

Giovanni clapped his hands. 'I know! Everyone can now see your lovely eyes.'

Stepping out of the salon, Amelie felt lighter, there was a spring in her step, and she couldn't wait to see Brendan's reaction – he couldn't fail to love her new image. There was still time to pop into the supermarket to buy a ready meal and a bottle of wine. Brendan would join her for a small glass when he got home.

It was ten o'clock before Brendan unlocked the door to their apartment. He threw his sports bag on the floor and poured himself a glass of milk from the fridge. Popping into the lounge, he kissed Amelie on top of her head. 'I'm whacked! Business is booming; I might need to take on a couple of trainers to help me out.'

Amelie stood up and smiled at her fiancé; she was excited to see his reaction to her new hairstyle. Brendan finished his milk. 'Another early start for me in the morning, I'm afraid. I need to be at the gym by six. I'll head off to bed now. Night.'

Amelie spun round and sank back down on the sofa. How dare he not even look at her properly? He was far too self-absorbed to notice her at all. Amelie poured the small glass of wine she had left out for him into hers. The amazing thing was that she wasn't annoyed. She reached for her purse and took out the drawing of the Christmas tree. It was a beautiful tree, with lots of baubles and presents underneath. There was a star on top and snow in the background. When Amelie closed her eyes, she could imagine the pencil sketch come to life – it was a magnificent scene when it was in colour.

Excitement bubbled through Amelie's veins. Why would someone be keen to change her mindset on Christmas? Would the artist be at the conference again this year? Amelie ran a hand through her soft, silky hair. She got up and turned the lights out. It was best to get an early night; tomorrow was going to be a long day.

3

THE ANNUAL CONFERENCE

Fifi was stunned. 'Oh my God, oh my God, oh my God!!!' She squealed with excitement before hugging Amelie. 'You look amazing! I can't believe it's really you. What did Brendan say?'

Amelie smiled. 'I'm pleased with it. Thanks for nagging me to get it done. Brendan didn't notice.'

'He didn't notice?! You are kidding me?'

Grant heard the commotion in the entrance hall. 'What's going on? Wow!! Who's the new delegate? We don't have a name badge.'

Amelie punched Grant's arm and laughed. 'Well, it's all your fault for making fun of my plaits. If you try to stitch me up again this year with doing an ice-breaker, I'll never forgive you. I want an easy day doing

14

some people watching. After the humiliation of last year, that's the least I deserve.'

Grant grinned. 'The only humiliating thing is that Featherlow Forbes' Top 100 all think you can't cook. No-one guessed you don't like Christmas. We were chatting to Chad last night in the wine bar, and he says he hopes your fiancé is good in the kitchen.'

'Chad Lagerfield didn't work out I don't like Christmas?'

'Not at all. He just thinks you're a rubbish cook. What does it matter? We only see him once a year.'

Amelie frowned. So, Action Man wasn't the artist. Probably just as well, that would have been awkward. Grant handed Amelie her name badge, and she placed her bag and conference folder on the edge of the table while she secured the pin in place. Amelie wished she hadn't chosen a silk blouse to wear; the badge flopped to one side. She fiddled with it as she looked at her reflection in the glass behind the welcome desk. A sudden jolt from behind sent her bag and folder flying onto the floor. Amelie spun round in annoyance.

A young man stood behind her with windswept blonde hair, a cycle helmet in his hand and a red perspiring face. 'Ooops, sorry! I never leave enough time to get to places. It's the first time I've been to one of these. I can see my badge over there. I'll grab it if I may.'

Amelie read the name on the badge: "Fabio". After pinning his badge onto his jacket pocket, the young man remembered his manners. 'Let me help you pick that up. It was my fault I bumped into you. Here – I'm not sure if your papers are in the right order. Sorry about that.'

The awkward intruder headed in the direction of the cloakrooms and Amelie sat down in an armchair to sort out her things. 'Well, if it's not Amelie. Pigtails one minute and a stylish crop the next.'

Amelie recognised the voice without even looking up. Felicity Furnleigh, Global Head of Marketing and Amelie's boss, had been given the nickname "the witch" by Fifi. 'Good morning, Felicity. Can I get you a coffee or anything?'

The witch patted Amelie's shoulder and bent down to whisper in her ear. 'I've just heard a jolly good rumour. Can you keep a secret?' Amelie nodded. 'There's a good chance old Lord Featherlow's stepping down. You know what that means don't you?' Amelie shook her head. 'The Chief Executive Officer position will become vacant. Of course, I'll take you with me as my Executive Assistant when that happens. Just keep schtum for now. Everything will fall into place soon enough.'

Amelie felt a tingle of fear creep up her spine. No way would she be going with the witch. Executive Assistant to the CEO was Grant's job. Poor Grant. Amelie may soon be getting a reprieve from the witch – or made redundant. Her heart sank; that wouldn't be good timing with the wedding coming up. Brendan would not be happy.

The name badges on the welcome desk were all taken, and Grant ushered the delegates into the main conference room. Amelie decided to sit in the back row – less chance of getting dragged onto the stage. Chad Lagerfield sat next to her. 'I like your new hair-do. So that's where you were last night instead of in the wine bar.'

Amelie blushed, and Grant rang the customary Featherlow Forbes hand-bell. That was enough to silence the audience. 'Ladies and Gentlemen, it gives me great pleasure to introduce the head of our team: Lord Featherlow.'

Lord Featherlow was, as ever, immaculately dressed. His silver hair shone under the spotlight, and his forever-tan was well-moisturised, eliminating all signs of lines and wrinkles. He held his arms in the air to encompass the rapturous applause. 'Thank you, thank you. If there's one thing I hold close to my heart that's family. You are all part of the Featherlow Forbes family, and for that, I afford you my sincerest gratitude.'

The Lord took hold of the notes Grant had placed on the podium and ripped them up. He scattered the pieces on the stage. 'This is a symbol. A symbol of times changing. My speech was written over a month ago. But two weeks ago, something amazing happened – I saw the light. I have only one person to thank for guiding me there, and that's my very dear and trusted colleague Felicity Furnleigh.' The Lord clapped, and the audience tentatively followed, wondering what they were clapping about.

The clapping ceased, and Lord Featherlow continued, 'Felicity reminded me of what's important in life. She made me realise I'm no spring chicken – I will soon turn seventy. Indeed, following the death of my beloved sister Foxy Forbes at the age of fifty-five, I'm very much on borrowed time. As you all know, Foxy was the brains behind our business. She had the vision and drive. I had the title that added some clout to a bespoke menswear company, but Foxy was the founder, the inspiration, the heart.'

The clapping started up again in memory of Foxy Forbes. This time it was wholehearted and lasted for several minutes. Lord Featherlow wiped away a tear. 'Thank you, thank you. It is with my firm belief in family that I want Featherlow Forbes to flourish for generations to come. I want all of you to be proud to work for our organisation and, to do that, you need a new leader. It's time for me to step down.'

There were gasps from the audience and a few stifled sobs. The witch polished her red talons against her skirt as she ran her acceptance speech over in her head. She was in such a zone that she was oblivious to what came next: 'From this moment, I will be leaving my role as your Chief Executive Officer and taking on a lesser role, in my eyes, as non-Executive Chairman. In simple terms, that means I will be stepping up to an overseeing role, rather than a hands-on one. Although, I'm sure I won't need to oversee very much.'

Felicity stood up and waited in the aisle. There were sunken hearts throughout the room, and Lord Featherlow's eyes twinkled. 'It gives me great pleasure to announce I am keeping things in the family. Please be upstanding to meet Fabio Forbes, my dearest nephew and Foxy's son.'

From his position in the back row, Chad noticed Felicity's knees crumble. He jumped up and shoved her back in her seat. The clapping had started again, and Fabio stood at the front of the stage, waiting to address the Featherlow Forbes team.

Amelie's eyes were on stalks. Surely this ungainly character couldn't take over from his uncle? Although, Fabio looked much more composed than when he'd just got off his bike. He seemed very young standing there at centre stage, but his demeanour portrayed inner confidence and keenness to be handed such a role.

The clapping ceased, and Fabio spoke. 'If you're surprised about this, then so am I. The first I heard about it was two weeks ago. All I can say is "thank you" to my uncle for having faith in me. I am sure many of you wonder what on earth is going on, but I promise you I will do my best to bring Featherlow Forbes into the next generation and beyond.'

More clapping – then the Featherlow Forbes bell. Grant spoke into the microphone. 'Thank you, Lord Featherlow and Fabio Forbes, it's now time for the first presentation for today from Chad Lagerfield, Head of Canadian Operations.'

*

At lunchtime, Fifi made a beeline for Amelie. 'Did you see Lord Featherlow rip up his speech? I couldn't take my eyes off Grant; he looked distraught. I know he'd put a lot of effort into pitching it just right for today's event. I think Lord Featherlow was rude.'

Amelie's eyes searched for Grant, who was rushing around between the caterers and the leadership team. He flashed a dimpled smile at Chad Lagerfield, then glanced over at Fifi who was now chatting to a waiter. A tingle crept up Amelie's spine; Fifi was right – he *was* upset. His hazel eyes were dull and, when he thought no-one was looking, his smile faded.

With Felicity Furnleigh's morning presentation over-running, lunch was cut to thirty minutes. Fifi nudged Amelie. 'Eat up! We'll need something to sustain us for this afternoon's team-building exercise. Grant tipped me off that we're going to be wearing overalls and doing some painting. Apparently, we're collectively going to produce a masterpiece to go on show at Head Office. I need some of that chocolate gateau before I can turn into the next Michelangelo.'

4

THE ANNUAL PARTY

When the day's activities were over, Amelie unlocked the door to her hotel room and collapsed onto the bed. What a whirlwind of events! Her new image had gone down well; all the compliments seemed genuine. The announcement about Lord Featherlow handing over the reins of the organisation to his nephew had come as somewhat of a shock; poor Felicity Furnleigh had survived the day in a daze. The news that Chad Lagerfield had only found out last night that Amelie didn't like Christmas was a bit of a disappointment. If he wasn't the artist, then who was?

It was six o'clock, and Fifi said she would knock for Amelie at six forty-five. There was just time for a quick shower and change before the Featherlow

Forbes annual party began. Amelie unzipped her overnight bag and pulled out her trusty cream cocktail dress. She had worn it on many occasions, it didn't crease and was simple enough not to direct attention towards her. Her hand touched the box beneath the dress, and a wave of guilt washed over her. In a fit of devilment against Brendan this morning, she'd packed her sparkly designer wedding shoes to wear this evening. Amelie sighed, she'd *have* to wear them now, she couldn't wear her flat black pumps.

*

Grant knocked for Fifi as soon as he was able to extract himself from the last lingering delegates in the conference room. Fifi was about to get in the shower; she told Grant to help himself to the minibar and to pour her a drink too. Showered and dressed, Fifi sashayed into the bedroom and sat down at the dressing table to do her makeup. 'OK, Grant McGuire, you can let it all out now. Did you know about Fabio Forbes taking over?'

Grant handed Fifi her drink. 'I knew nothing. What does that tell you?'

Fifi shrugged. 'That's it's all been kept top secret?'

'Exactly.'

'How will you feel working for Fabio?'

'That's just the point. Surely Fabio would have approached me by now if he wanted me to work for him. Just to introduce himself, or something. He had plenty of opportunities to speak to me today, but he avoided me. There's a very good chance I could be made redundant.'

Fifi shuddered. New boss, new ways – Grant had a point. Featherlow Forbes could be in for a shake-up. She hated to see Grant so desolate. 'I've promised to knock for Amelie in ten minutes. Why don't you go and get changed and we'll meet you down in the bar? If I get a chance to chat to Fabio tonight, I'll be singing your praises.'

*

Grant reached the bar before the girls. Lord Featherlow was seated next to Chad Lagerfield. As soon as he saw Grant, he stood up and walked towards him. 'Grant! Just the person. I need to speak to you, let's go outside.'

It was a bright September evening, and the men sat beside each other overlooking an ornamental pond. Grant's heart pounded. Lord Featherlow spoke in a low voice. 'I am sure this has all come as a shock to you. It certainly has to me. Just two weeks ago, I became aware of some unethical behaviour within our business. I can't say what until I have more details. The best way I can get to the bottom of things is from afar.

Fabio has agreed to help me. In fact, the only two people I can trust at the moment are my nephew and my Executive Assistant.

Grant felt a warm feeling encompass his body. 'I'll do whatever you need me to, Lord Featherlow.'

'I know that, Grant. You are going to be key in all of this. You will be my eyes and ears. To the outside world, you will be working for Fabio here in London, but I will be in the background controlling things from Featherlow Manor.'

Grant grinned. 'This all sounds very exciting!'

Lord Featherlow frowned. 'It will be a challenging time and potentially dangerous. You will need to keep your wits about you at all times.'

Grant's head jerked at the sound of whistling coming from behind. He stood up to the sight of his new "boss" striding towards them. 'Grant McGuire, I believe! I'm Fabio. Very pleased to meet you.'

Lord Featherlow stood up and placed a hand on Fabio's arm. 'I have briefed Grant. We need to get through this evening without raising suspicion. I'll meet you both in the office at nine in the morning. I'll clear my desk, then head off home to set up my work station.'

*

Fifi and Amelie studied the seating plan for dinner. Amelie was seated next to Fabio and Fifi was on Chad Lagerfield's table at the other side of the room. Fifi tutted. 'We need to switch places. I've promised Grant I'll do everything I can to stop him from being made redundant.' Fifi tottered off into the dining room to move the place names around.

At seven-thirty Grant rang the Featherlow Forbes bell as a signal for everyone to take their places for dinner. He'd prepared the table plans himself, so was surprised to see Fifi wandering over to sit next to Fabio and Amelie head for the other side of the room. What were those two playing at? After ensuring everyone was seated, Grant headed to his table and was dismayed to see that *his* place name had been moved; he was now sitting next to Felicity Furnleigh.

Felicity gave him one of her sugary smiles. 'Grant! How convenient. You must share with me your thoughts on today's announcement. Of course, Lord Featherlow has kept me fully briefed on proceedings, but I just wanted to hear your opinion on all the changes.'

Amelie had a clear view of Chad as he was sitting opposite her on their table of ten. He flashed his white smile her way whenever he came up for air from keeping conversation with the very attentive ladies either side of him. The waiter leant over Amelie. 'More potatoes, Madam?'

Amelie smiled up at him. 'No, thank you. I'd better not.' The waiter's deep blue eyes bore into hers. Amelie blushed. She was undoubtedly getting noticed since her makeover. She felt the newness of her wedding shoes on her feet and tried not to scuff them against a table leg.

Fifi made the most of her opportunity with Fabio. 'Grant McGuire is an excellent Executive Assistant. I know your uncle has valued him highly over the years. From my point of view, he makes my life on reception so much easier by always advising me when visitors are due, or if he's expecting any deliveries. He always has a ready smile. He's courteous and charming, and he doesn't treat me like the lowest of the low. He treats every member of the Featherlow Forbes family with the utmost respect.'

Fabio held up his glass to clink Fifi's. 'OK, you've sold him to me. I'll keep Grant on as my Executive Assistant. He can't get a more glowing reference than the one you've just given.'

Fifi blushed and felt her heart fly. She wanted to lean over and hug Fabio but knew that wouldn't be appropriate. A waiter picked up Fifi's empty plate, and discretely removed the drawing beneath it.

Grant was relieved the meal was coming to an end.

He extracted himself from Felicity's intense scrutiny and, bell in hand, climbed onto the stage where a band had been setting up behind the curtains. He poked his head through. 'Everyone ready?' There were smiles and nods, and Grant rang the bell.

'It's time for the party to begin!' Grant pressed a button on a remote control, the curtains opened, and the band burst into life.

Chad stood up and strode around the table to ask Amelie for a dance. How could she refuse, without looking rude? Her shoes felt tight; luckily, Chad wasn't aware as he glanced down at them admiringly. How bad that the first dance in her wedding shoes would be with this model of a man who was swinging her around with glee. The only consolation Amelie could find to ease her conscience was that the dance with Brendan would be much different. He had agreed to just one dance as long as it was slow, and they just shuffled around. At least her shoes would be comfortable by her wedding day; it had been a good decision to wear them.

Fifi excused herself from Fabio and hauled Grant onto the dancefloor. 'I've done it! I've given you a good reference and Fabio is keeping you on as his Executive Assistant!'

Grant suppressed a chuckle. He felt touched by Fifi's loyalty. 'Really? That's great! I owe you one.'

Amelie made her excuses and returned to her room by eleven. She'd had a good time this evening. The news that Grant was keeping his job as Executive Assistant to the CEO was brilliant. The only downside was that Felicity Furnleigh was sure to be like a bear with a sore head for the next few weeks.

5

UNDER NEW MANAGEMENT

After an early breakfast, Fifi, Grant and Amelie headed into the office for eight-thirty. None of them wanted to be late on Fabio's first day. The security guard on reception handed Amelie an envelope, and she shoved it into her bag while Grant held the lift door open.

It was the start of a new era for Featherlow Forbes. Amelie was pleased that Grant was embracing the change; he'd worked for Lord Featherlow for ten years. Fabio was a completely different character to his uncle; Amelie pushed any reservations she had of Fabio's ability to manage the company to the back of her mind. When he rushed past her desk, with his messy hair and cycle helmet in hand, she smiled at him.

Fabio waved. 'Good morning! Surprisingly cold outside this morning. It'll soon be Christmas.'

A tingle trickled down Amelie's spine. Surely not! Fabio wasn't even at the event last year. Amelie couldn't resist reaching inside her purse and having a quick look at the Christmas tree. No – Fabio wouldn't be the artist; she was sure of that. Felicity strolled out of the lift as Amelie reached for a paperknife to open the envelope she'd received on her way in this morning.

'Morning, Felicity. Did you sleep well?'

Felicity struggled to undo the buttons on her red mohair coat. Her talons were useful for finger-pointing and scaring her weaker-willed colleagues, but the majority of the time Amelie thought they put her at a disadvantage. Felicity couldn't even press the lift button without using a pen.

Felicity smiled. 'I was up rather late, I'm afraid. Fabio was keen to get my stance on things. He was very inquisitive. I have a feeling he's going to need me immensely. My knowledge and experience will be invaluable to him.'

Amelie gasped and threw a hand to her mouth. Felicity glared at her. 'What's up with you?'

'Nothing. Just nothing.'

Amelie rushed into the Ladies cloakroom and opened the envelope again. It contained a drawing. This time there was a roaring fire with two stockings hanging from the mantelpiece. A mince pie, carrot and what looked like a glass of whisky were next to the fireplace.

A chuckle bubbled up from inside Amelie's stomach. She hoped the fire would be out before Santa came down the chimney. What was happening? Why was she even thinking about Christmas? She'd made a promise to Brendan. This was all really silly. Who was playing jokes on her?

Lord Featherlow marched from the lift to the glass-walled boardroom where Fabio and Grant were waiting. He closed the door behind him. The staff in the office could see him pacing around, scratching his head.

'I received another note this morning. It disturbed me greatly.'

Grant raised his eyebrows. 'Another note? What did the first one say?'

'The first one said: There's corruption in the leadership team. Watch your back.'

Fabio's eyes widened. 'And today's note?'

'Things will come to a head at Christmas.'

Grant scribbled on his notepad. 'That gives us just over twelve weeks to get to the bottom of things. Where do we start?'

Fabio leant back in his chair. 'I made a good start last night. If there's corruption in the leadership team, then Felicity Furnleigh will be involved. That woman is as evil as they come. She wants the CEO position without a doubt. She feels she's got rid of uncle, and now she's trying to get her claws into me. She made a powerful attempt at trying to scare me off.'

Lord Featherlow was intrigued. 'What did she say?'

'She said that you're an old codger, I'm just a whippersnapper who has no idea about menswear, and that she can save me from a dramatic fall if I make her my right-hand woman.'

Lord Featherlow stood with hands on hips and glared through the glass wall at Felicity who had just dropped her mobile phone due to her talons and was bending over to pick it up. 'I should have fired her years ago.'

Grant piped up. 'Why didn't you? You certainly have cause to fire her now – she can't go around speaking about you like that.'

Lord Featherlow sat down. 'It's a classic case of keeping your enemies close.'

Fabio nodded. 'I agree. Felicity will lead us to the brains behind whatever's planned to happen at Christmas. I'll act like the clown she thinks I am. That'll trap her.'

*

It was lunchtime before Lord Featherlow said his "goodbyes" and walked out of the building with a heavy heart. His chauffeur held the limousine door open, and Lord Featherlow strode past the homeless man sitting on the pavement without further thought.

Amelie noticed the poor hooded man as she dashed past on her way to the sandwich shop. When she returned, she dropped a filled baguette into his lap. That was much better for him than loose change. She waited for Felicity to exit via the revolving door before making her way back into the building.

Fifi was standing on tiptoe behind the reception desk straining her neck. 'Amelie! Did you see that? The witch gave the homeless man a note; he's reading it now. Why would she do that?'

Amelie watched the man put the note in his pocket before taking a bite out of the baguette. 'How strange? She was probably giving him a written warning about taking up pavement space outside Featherlow Forbes. He won't look good sitting outside. Felicity's big on image.'

Fifi gasped. 'You guessed right. Look! He's moving on. If there's one thing you can say about Felicity Furnleigh, it's that she always gets the job done. No-one stands in her way.' Amelie raised her eyes to the ceiling and headed for the lift. She should have at least twenty minutes to eat her sandwich in peace before Felicity returned to crack the whip.

With everything quiet on reception, Fifi reached into her bag and pulled out a chocolate bar. Boot Camp was starting on Monday. Why on earth had she signed up for it? She could think of no worse way to spend an evening. Still, the fact that Brendan hadn't even noticed Amelie's makeover made it all worthwhile. The sooner Fifi got closer to him, the better; there was something about him that gave her the creeps. In Fifi's mind, Brendan was not all that he seemed.

6

BOOT CAMP

Monday morning arrived, and Amelie headed straight for the reception desk. Fifi smiled at her friend. 'So, how did the wedding dress fitting go?'

'It went well. The dressmaker only has a few nips and tucks to make. I'll need to ensure I don't pile on the pounds before Christmas.'

Fifi laughed. 'You never put on weight. I wish I were like you.'

Amelie blushed. 'Anyway, Brendan is starting a new Boot Camp tonight. That means I have Monday nights free until the wedding. Do you fancy going to the wine bar after work?'

Fifi would much rather go to the wine bar than the gym. She took a deep breath and just managed to keep her willpower intact. 'Sorry, I can't make tonight.'

Amelie smiled. 'Never mind. We can meet up next week instead.'

Grant was at the drinks machine on the fourth floor. Amelie walked over to join him. 'I've got a free night tonight. Fancy going for a drink after work?'

That jogged Grant's memory to the fact that Fifi would be attending Brendan's Boot Camp. He couldn't help but smile at the thought of it. Fifi would do anything for her friends. 'Of course. Let's aim to leave the office by six.'

Fabio joined them at the drinks machine. He wasn't flushed with helmet in hand. Instead, he looked calm and composed, and his blonde hair was immaculate. 'What's this? Are you planning a drink after work? Any problem if I come along?'

*

Fifi was starving by eight o'clock. She hadn't dared eat anything in case a full stomach limited her ability to perform to Brendan's commands. Her heart sank when she walked into the gym to find it full of men. That wasn't a good start. She strode over to Brendan. 'I thought this was supposed to be a ladies group?'

Brendan shrugged his shoulders. 'I've got a business to run. Only two females signed up.'

The door swung open, and Felicity Furnleigh jogged in, dressed in pink lycra. 'Sorry I'm late everyone. Busy job. Busy me.' Felicity's mouth fell open at the sight of Fifi in her black leggings and T-shirt.

Fifi didn't know whether to laugh or cry. To make matters worse, she could see Rizor Rochester out of the corner of her eye. Featherlow Forbes' Global Head of Sales was instantly recognisable due to his bright red hair and piercing green eyes. Fifi cringed; things were turning from bad to worse. She just wanted to run outside and head for the wine bar.

Brendan clapped his hands. 'I like to bring some competition to my Boot Camps. We'll be working in two teams. I'll measure each team on weight loss and performance. Most of you will be building muscle, so performance is key. You need to think "WIN". The first thing you need to win is the captaincy of your team. The first two to climb to the top of the wall bars down the far end of the room will be named as team captains.' Brendan blew a whistle, and the most competitive of the group members flew off at a pace.

There were two clear winners: Rizor Rochester and an odd-looking guy called Spacey. It was a shock to everyone *he* won that challenge. Spacey was heavy around the middle, wore tracksuit bottoms and a sweatshirt and refused to take off his beanie hat. He needed a good shave, but apart from that, he was quick. He'd beaten Rizor by at least ten seconds.

No-one was more surprised than Brendan at Spacey's athleticism. 'OK. Spacey and Rizor choose your teams. Spacey has first choice.'

Fifi's knees buckled when Spacey chose her first. It was pretty obvious that Rizor would choose Felicity, after that the choosing went backwards and forwards until there were six on each team.

The next hour passed in a blur for Fifi. She kept an eye on the clock on the wall throughout the session. As soon as she was released, she staggered out of the gym straight to the wine bar. It was after nine; no-one would notice what she was wearing if she could sneak in and squeeze in next to Grant. Amelie would have headed off home by now.

Fifi was relieved to find Grant still there but perturbed that Fabio was with him. Needs must though, she edged onto a stool next to Grant and gasped: 'I need a wine.'

Fabio summoned a waiter. 'Allow me.'

Grant noticed Fifi's glazed eyes. 'You look in a state of shock. I don't think Boot Camp suits you.'

Fifi wiped her forehead with a tissue. 'I have just had the most dreadful experience. You'll never guess what happened.'

Fabio was intrigued. 'I need to catch up here. I take it you've been to the gym.'

Fifi nodded. 'I certainly have. And so have two members of the leadership team. Neither of them needs to lose weight or go to a cheap backstreet gym. It was bizarre. Can you believe the witch kept popping into the manager's office for a rest? Rizor nearly exploded at one point; he was desperate to beat Spacey, but our team won all the challenges. Rizor's not a good loser.'

Grant glanced at Fabio, who was keen to hear more. 'Who's the witch?'

Fifi blushed. 'Felicity Furnleigh. No offence, but she's not always nice.'

Fabio smiled and nodded. 'Who's Spacey?'

'Some really fit guy who doesn't look fit at all. He chose me to be on his team.'

Fabio topped up Fifi's wine glass and stared at Grant as he spoke. 'So, to summarise your evening, Fifi, you've joined a Boot Camp that was also attended by our Global Heads of Marketing and Sales. The other strange occurrence was that a fit guy, who doesn't look the part, was keen to get the better of our colleagues. The fit guy also chose you to be on his team.'

Fifi was calming down after her nightmare experience. 'That about sums it up. I won't be going again.'

Fabio leant forward with pleading eyes. 'You must go again, Fifi. We need you to. I, err, mean that it won't look good to the leadership team if they last longer than you. Why don't you treat it as a bit of fun? If you go again next week, we'll meet you here at the same time. I'll have the wine ready, and you can update us on progress.'

Fifi thought that was strange but who was she to complain? Fabio was showing a great deal of interest in her after-work activities. Fifi couldn't forget the real reason she was putting herself through this though and next week she would pay more attention to Brendan, she must be able to unravel something about him that would stop the wedding.

7

A MASTER OF DISGUISE

By the end of October, shops and restaurants in London were glittering with Christmas decorations. Amelie window-shopped with a heavy heart. Brendan had refused to go out with her since the beginning of the month; from when the first Christmas tree went on display in Fifi's hairdressing salon. That meant for three months every year of their married life, Brendan would go into hibernation. Was he worth making that sacrifice for? Amelie was beginning to doubt it.

It was bright and crisp that Saturday morning, the sky was blue, the pavements were frosty, and a small café up a cobbled side street made a welcome sight. Amelie peered through the window and stopped in her tracks; Felicity Furnleigh was sitting at a table in the back corner with a man. Amelie gasped, and a scream threatened to escape her. Suddenly a gloved hand clasped her mouth, and a strong arm pulled her away from the window.

Amelie began kicking and punching her captor until he turned her round to look into his deep blue eyes. It was the homeless man. He was wearing the same navy hoodie. She hadn't noticed his eyes when she'd given him the baguette, but she'd seen those eyes before – they were the same as the waiter's at the hotel when he offered her extra potatoes at the Featherlow Forbes annual party. The homeless man didn't look too dishevelled close-up, and he smelt of expensive aftershave.

Amelie's knees were weak, and she let the man hold her up. 'I've just had a terrible shock. My boss is in that café – with my fiancé!'

The man smiled at her with kind eyes. 'I know. I've been keeping track of them. Things are coming to a head. I was trying not to get you involved, but now I need to keep you from danger. Come with me. I will explain everything.'

The man led Amelie through one side street to another before removing his hooded jacket. He combed his fingers through his shiny black hair and headed straight for The Fortescue Tower. 'Don't be alarmed. I have a suite here as a base. It's the one place in London my father won't visit. He can't stand the building. I think it was something to do with Featherlow Forbes not winning the tender to design the uniforms. My father can become very closed off if something doesn't go his way. I live to tell the tale of that.'

Amelie was dumbstruck. She was now in a plush suite with fantastic views over London with a man whom she thought was homeless. Amelie had even bought him a baguette! She was sure the eyes were the same as the waiter's, but *he'd* had light brown hair. As Amelie wandered around the living room, she caught sight of a sketchbook on a desk. Her hand went to touch it just as the mystery man entered the room with a butler in tow. 'I'm ravenous. You must be too. If you let me order the Christmas platter for lunch, I'll confess everything.'

Amelie nodded, and the butler left the room. 'You were a waiter at the Featherlow Forbes annual party, weren't you? You had different hair.'

'Great detective work! It was a wig. I see you've noticed my sketchbook. So, I'm afraid to say; it's hands up from me. I'm the artist.'

Amelie held her head in her hands. 'But why? I'm so confused.'

'Please take a seat, and I'll tell all.'

Amelie sat on a sofa with a straight back and her hands in her lap.

'My name's Freddie Featherlow, and I'm Lord Featherlow's estranged son. I'm thirty-five years' old and was destined to take over Featherlow Forbes one day. My younger cousin, Fabio, has no interest whatsoever in working in menswear. He's doing a favour for my father who is currently in a predicament about who he can trust.'

The butler entered the room with a tray of turkey sandwiches, pigs in blankets, cheese straws and mince pies. There was also a carafe of mulled wine. Freddie's smile lit up the room. 'They look after me here – all of my favourite things! It reminds me of home at Christmastime. There's nothing better than a big family Christmas.'

Freddie tucked into a sandwich, and Amelie asked the most obvious question: 'Why are you estranged from your father?'

Freddie's smile was now tinged with sadness. 'It happened five years ago. I was due to get married to a beautiful woman. Not only was she stunningly gorgeous, but she was also mega-wealthy. Our wedding was planned for Christmas Eve.'

Amelie gasped. '*I'm* getting married on Christmas Eve!'

Freddie shook his head. 'Not if I have anything to do with it.'

Amelie glared at this confident man who was trying to stop her from getting married. He certainly had some cheek. Her head was thumping, and redness was creeping up from her neck onto her face. She felt extremely uncomfortable and annoyed.

Freddie noticed her awkwardness, what he was about to tell Amelie would come as a shock. He needed to do it sooner rather than later. 'Your wedding is planned as a decoy to a heist on Christmas Eve. Brendan won't be turning up; he'll be in collusion with Felicity Furnleigh and her associates. You're better off without him. Why marry a man who doesn't adore Christmas?'

Amelie opened her mouth to speak, but no words came out. She felt numb. Surely she knew Brendan better than anyone? Amelie jumped up and stormed over to a window. Tears welled in her eyes before her whole body shook with anger.

Freddie gave her a handkerchief. 'I know this will come as a shock to you.'

Amelie blew her nose. 'I've known Brendan my whole life. I trust him. Why should I believe you? How do you know about a heist on Christmas Eve?'

'I've overheard them at the gym. I haven't worked out yet what they're planning to steal; I just need to ensure my family is protected.' Amelie burst into tears again.

Freddie frowned; he hadn't expected Amelie to be so upset. By giving her the drawings, he'd tried to make her realise there was so much more to life than Brendan could offer. Freddie knew, deep down, the sketches had ignited a flicker of doubt inside Amelie. Brendan's association with Felicity Furnleigh would surely extinguish any remaining feelings Amelie had for the spineless loser who wouldn't realise how lucky he was until Amelie was gone.

Freddie placed an arm around Amelie's shoulders and moved her towards a telescope before checking his watch. 'Have a look through there. Don't move it. It's pointing in the right direction.' Amelie looked through the telescope to the sight of Brendan's gym. Freddie continued, 'It's two o'clock now, and the gym is shut. Unusual for a Saturday, don't you think? Anyway, you will shortly see a white van pull up outside.'

Amelie shivered. 'I can see it.'

Freddie rubbed his hands together. 'Great! Move over. I need to have a look.' Five minutes later, Freddie extracted himself from the telescope and punched the air. 'Brendan and Felicity have just taken delivery of the stolen goods.'

'How do you know the goods are stolen?'

'Because they're mine.'

Amelie blew her nose again. 'This all sounds very complicated. I'm struggling to keep up.'

'It *is* very complicated, but you'll have the full picture soon enough. It just means you need to spend the whole afternoon with me and, when you're fully briefed, we can celebrate by going out on the town for dinner.'

Amelie's stomach somersaulted at that thought; what was happening to her? Could she trust Freddie Featherlow? If she were honest with herself, she had been having doubts about marrying Brendan; he was the least attentive bridegroom you could imagine. Now Amelie knew why – he wasn't planning on marrying her at all.

Amelie's shock was turning to intrigue. 'What happened about *your* wedding?'

Freddie's eyes twinkled. 'I did a runner before the bride arrived. My father was furious and disowned me there and then. My decision proved very awkward for him in social circles. I guess by removing me from the family, he was able to save face with his colleagues, customers and the higher echelons of society he rubs shoulders with on a daily basis.'

Amelie's heart went out to Freddie. 'Why did you do a runner?'

Freddie shrugged. 'Because I didn't love her.'

8

MORE CONFESSIONS

With just one pig in blanket and two cheese straws left on the Christmas platter, Freddie wiped his mouth and tried to put his mission in an order that would make sense to Amelie. He leant back in an armchair and closed his eyes. 'Where do I begin?'

Intrigue was keeping Amelie focused. How did Brendan get involved with all of this? Was their proposed wedding really a sham? Freddie sat forward and rested his arms on his legs as he locked eyes with Amelie. 'It all started a year ago when I first met you.'

Amelie's eyes widened. 'Me?'

'Yes, you. I've kept in contact with Chad Lagerfield over the last five years – he's one of the good guys on the leadership team. I was in London at the time of the Featherlow Forbes annual conference and met up with Chad the night before. I couldn't resist staying around the next day to see how my father was fairing up, that's when I posed as a waiter for the first time. I have an old friend who works in the kitchen, and he was keen to help me out. I didn't do a full shift.'

'Didn't your father recognise you?'

'Not with that wig. Anyway, I saw your embarrassment about getting dragged onto the stage and worked out right away that you didn't like Christmas.'

'How did you guess?'

'You were wearing an engagement ring, and you gave Fifi a box of cupcakes you'd made the previous night. It was easy to work out what the untruth was after that.'

'So, you drew me a Christmas tree.'

'Correct. After that, things started to get out of control. Chad tipped me off about Felicity Furnleigh planning a takeover of the business and trying to overthrow my father. I couldn't let that happen, so I've been keeping a close eye on her.'

'But she didn't pull it off. Your father has put Fabio Forbes in charge.'

'That's only a temporary fix. Fabio won't stay around for long.'

'So, Felicity's takeover bid failed and she's planning a robbery instead?'

Freddie glanced at Amelie. 'That's not technically correct. Felicity has been planning the heist on Christmas Eve since March. She wanted to achieve both.'

Amelie threw her hands to her mouth. 'Brendan proposed to me in March. He insisted we get married on Christmas Eve. It really is true, isn't it? He never intended marrying me.'

Freddie hung his head. 'I'm so sorry, Amelie.'

'Why did you draw me a picture of a fireplace with two stockings hanging from the mantelpiece?'

Freddie gave a wry smile. 'That one caused me a problem. I put it under your plate at the dinner and then realised you had changed places with Fifi. I still got it to you, though. By that stage, I was desperate for you to break things off with Brendan. I knew by then that he was corrupt. I thought you would see the picture and realise that if you married him, you would never have stockings hanging from your fireplace for the rest of your life.'

A lightbulb switched on in Amelie's head. 'Felicity

Furnleigh gave you a note. You read it before eating my baguette!'

'That's correct. I still have it. I'll get it for you.'

Freddie returned with the note inside a clear plastic wallet. 'Her fingerprints are on it; we may need it as evidence.'

Amelie read the note: *Jewels to the gym. 2 pm Saturday 31st October.*

'That's today! What jewels?'

Freddie grinned. 'It's a classic case of how to catch a thief. Give them bait and wait for them to pounce.'

'But Felicity's not a thief.'

'She tried to steal my father's job. That's a thief in my eyes. She also thrives on corruption. Goodness knows what she's got up to in the past. Anyway, let's focus on the here and now. In my disguise as a homeless man, I approached her one day to advise I had access to jewels if she was interested. She bit my hand off – paid me one hundred pounds for my time and said she'd contact me to advise where and when to drop them off.'

'Where did YOU get the jewels?'

'They're from my collection and worth much more than one hundred pounds. Before you ask – I've been designing men's jewellery for the last five years and doing very well I might add.' Freddie lowered his eyes. 'I hope my father would be proud of me.'

Amelie smiled. 'Oh, I'm sure he will be. He cannot fail to welcome you back to the family when he realises how hard you've tried to protect him. Why don't you expose the leadership team now? You've got enough evidence.'

Freddie frowned. 'I need to know exactly what they're planning for Christmas Eve. I fear my father may be in danger. Felicity Furnleigh won't stop at bringing him down. You could play a key part in helping me if you wish.'

'What would I need to do?'

'You need to go along with your wedding knowing very well that Brendan's not going to turn up. I know it's a big ask, but at the end of the day, I'm doing you a favour. When I'm back in the family fold I'll find you a replacement for Brendan, I promise. My father has contacts in high places; he'll help with finding you a good man.'

How could Amelie resist such an offer? The short amount of time she'd spent with Freddie had shocked her to the core. She'd had more excitement in one afternoon with Lord Featherlow's son than in a lifetime of knowing Brendan. 'OK, I'm in.'

'Great!' Freddie stared at Amelie as he ran a hand through his shiny black hair. 'Promise not to be cross with her, but you should know about Fifi. She's joined Brendan's Boot Camp on Monday evenings. She hates it. She's just doing it because her instinct tells her that Brendan's corrupt. She'd be livid with me if she knew I was already on the case.'

'Fifi knows you?'

'Well, yes and no. Fifi knows me as "Spacey". Don't laugh; it's just another disguise. I'm hoping to find out what's planned for Christmas Eve by keeping my ear to the ground in the gym. Not literally I might add!'

Amelie giggled. 'I can't believe Fifi's going to the gym to spy on Brendan!'

'She's a good girl, that one – a true friend. Goodness, is that the time? We'd best make a move. Mind if I wear a beanie hat?'

'Where are we going?'

'How does a riverboat cruise before dinner sound? I'll take my hat off in the restaurant later. I know a nice little place my father definitely won't frequent.'

9

THE CONSPIRATORS

On Monday morning Amelie found a sealed envelope propped up on her desk. She recognised the writing from the last one, and her heart leapt. Felicity hadn't arrived yet, so Amelie opened the envelope and took out the drawing of a winking Father Christmas lifting the lid on a box full of jewels. Amelie chuckled and put the drawing with the others in her purse.

Fabio and Grant were in the boardroom surrounded by empty coffee cups. They seemed frazzled. Amelie knocked on the door before entering. 'It looks like you two were in early, can I get you some more coffee?'

Fabio leant back in his chair. 'Come in, Amelie, and shut the door behind you. Please take a seat.' Amelie sat down, and Fabio continued, 'Grant tells me you can be trusted. What I am going to tell you now should go no further than this room.'

Amelie's eyes widened. 'I won't tell a soul.'

Fabio frowned. 'We have reason to believe that Felicity Furnleigh is planning to abduct Lord Featherlow on Christmas Eve.'

Amelie's mouth flew open. 'What?! How did you find that out?'

'Grant was tipped off by some homeless guy yesterday. We've checked our CCTV on the dates and times he gave us, and Felicity was seen either speaking to the guy or passing him a note.'

'Are you going to tell the police?'

Fabio shook his head. 'The homeless guy gave Grant an idea. He said that Felicity isn't as sharp as she looks. We need to turn things around and give her something much more appealing to steal than an old man.'

Amelie snorted and covered her face with her hands. Grant stared at her. 'This isn't funny, Amelie.'

Amelie tried to think quickly. What would help Freddie? 'I'm sorry, but this all sounds bizarre. The priority here is to ensure that Lord Featherlow is safe on Christmas Eve. He'll need protection.'

Fabio raised his hands in the air. 'What do you suggest?'

'Why don't you organise a big event and ensure that Lord Featherlow is at the centre of it? You could splash out on the security budget as a precaution, and someone needs to shadow Felicity at all times.'

Grant frowned. 'But what can Felicity steal that would be appealing to her?'

Amelie had a brainwave. 'Jewellery. I have a friend who designs men's jewellery. We could have a Featherlow Forbes Christmas Spectacular with models bringing sparkle to the best time of the year!'

Grant stared at Amelie. 'But you don't like Christmas.'

Amelie lowered her eyes. 'I won't be there. I'll be at my wedding.'

Fabio rubbed his hands together. 'I think that's a great idea. We can hold the event at Featherlow Manor. My uncle tightened up on security when he bought those gold bars last year. Please ask your friend to come into the office, so that we can see her collection. A joint venture with us could be lucrative for both parties.'

Amelie stuttered. 'It ... it's not a "her". I'll need to check with him if he feels my idea is appropriate. Leave it with me. I'll get back to you.'

Amelie returned to her desk. Felicity was on the phone. Amelie was taken aback to see the witch's chunky fingers flashing with large sparkly rings – rings Amelie hadn't seen before. Amelie screwed her eyes up at her boss while she wasn't looking. She would get her comeuppance sooner rather than later.

Amelie reached into her bag for her phone. Freddie had beaten her to it. He'd sent a text message asking her to meet him at The Fortescue Tower at lunchtime.

*

Freddie poured the tea. 'You did what?!'

'I suggested that Featherlow Forbes holds a Christmas Spectacular on Christmas Eve and that they use your jewellery. Trust me – Fabio loved the idea. He even suggested they hold the event at Featherlow Manor as your father has stepped up security since he bought some gold bars last year.'

Freddie punched the air before throwing himself on the sofa and hugging Amelie. 'You did it! You found the missing piece of the jigsaw!'

Amelie blushed. 'I don't understand. I thought you'd be worried about Felicity Furnleigh abducting your father.'

Freddie jumped up and paced around the room. 'Oh, that was just a ploy. I made that bit up. I wanted

Fabio to check the CCTV and see that Felicity was conspiring with me. I didn't expect it to lead to the fact that my father has invested in gold bars. That explains everything.'

'What do you mean?'

'Fifi did me a huge favour at the gym last week. She hung around after most people had left and tried to chat up Brendan.'

'What???'

'Don't worry; he turned her down. I could tell she was gutted. She's just desperately trying to stop you marrying him. Grant's in on the act too. Neither of them feels you're suited to Brendan. They both think you could do much better. And, of course, they're right.'

Freddie winked, and Amelie blushed. 'You've gone off track. How did Fifi chatting up Brendan help you?'

'I managed to have a rummage around in his office and came across a sketch of a gold bar giving its dimensions and weight.'

Amelie gasped. 'So, Felicity and Rizor know about your father's gold bars, and they've roped Brendan in to do the muscle work during the heist on Christmas Eve.'

Freddie scratched his head as he continued to pace.

'I do believe that's it. All we need to do now is catch them in the act.'

10

MONDAY EVENING LIAISONS

Six weeks into Boot Camp and Fifi had lost a stone. She was amazed at how fit she felt. She didn't put it down to Brendan's expertise; it was Spacey that challenged her every week. Fifi wanted to do well for his team. He had such kind blue eyes. She was surprised that he didn't appear to be losing any weight – he was still chunky around the middle.

Freddie carried out the circuit training with vigour; he was sweltering beneath his padded bodysuit. Rizor was competitive each week, but with Felicity on his team, he never won any of the challenges. Rizor's patience was beginning to run out. As Featherlow Forbes' Global Head of Sales, he wasn't used to losing. He'd won the tender for four lucrative contracts in just the last week. His bonus would go through the roof at

Christmas. Suddenly, Felicity's underhand games no longer seemed appealing. Rizor wanted out.

After losing the latest challenge to Spacey's team, Rizor stormed out of the gym. Felicity rushed after him. 'Where are you going?'

'I'm done! I want no more to do with this. I'm requesting a meeting with Fabio Forbes first thing in the morning. He needs to know what you're up to.'

'But Rizor! You're part of this too.'

'No, I'm not. I was just keeping an eye on you to get enough evidence to nail you. Well, consider yourself well and truly nailed! If you'd made the slightest bit of effort with Boot Camp, then things may have been different. Your complacency has turned me into a loser. And, trust me, Rizor Rochester is no loser.'

A stunned Brendan rushed out of the gym to join the bickering pair. The remaining ten Boot Camp participants communicated by raised eyebrows, stifled sniggers, and nods in the direction of the open door. There was a row going on between the Lady in Pink Lycra and the captain of the losing team.

Fifi nudged Spacey. 'I think Felicity's got Rizor's back up. He won't be amused our team keeps winning all the tasks. He's very competitive. In my opinion, Felicity isn't taking things as seriously as us. Serves them right they never win anything.'

Brendan returned to a sea of expectant faces. He cleared his throat and shuffled his feet. 'We've just lost two Boot Camp participants, and I can't run it with less than twelve. I'm sorry, but we need to call it a day. I'll refund you for the final six weeks.'

One participant put his hand in the air. 'I'm sure I can find a couple of mates to make up the numbers next week.'

Brendan shook his head. 'There's no point; it's all off. I'm cancelling it.'

The sniggers from the participants turned to disgruntled mutters and raised eyes. One-by-one they exited the building. Spacey linked his arm through Fifi's as they lagged behind the group. He was holding her back to witness Felicity Furnleigh creeping into Brendan's office in a flood of tears.

Once they were outside, Spacey stared at her. 'I have a confession to make.' Fifi raised her eyebrows, and Spacey lifted his sweatshirt to reveal the padding. He then pulled at his unkempt beard which left glue marks on his handsome face. Fifi threw her hands to her mouth.

'My name's not Spacey. I'm Freddie Featherlow. Lord Featherlow's estranged son. I have been trying to win my father's respect by becoming a hero. But Rizor Rochester has just put an end to that. You could say he's the winner in the end.'

Fifi gasped. 'I don't know what you mean.'

Freddie sighed. 'It's a long story. It's been nice meeting you, Fifi. You're a good friend to Amelie. Don't worry about her marrying Brendan. That's never going to happen.'

Freddie clasped his sports bag in one hand and waved to Fifi with the other. He turned into a side street and disappeared out of sight.

There was only one thing for it – Fifi needed to get to the wine bar. Pushing her way through the boisterous crowd, she saw Amelie sitting with Fabio and Grant. They were surprised to see Fifi, who had turned up earlier than expected. She was as white as a sheet, and her hands were shaking. Grant helped her onto a stool. 'What on earth has happened?'

Fabio signalled to the waiter to bring wine, and Fifi stared at Amelie. 'Is there something you need to tell me?'

Amelie was stunned by Fifi's accusing glare. 'I … I don't know what you mean.'

Fifi sighed. 'OK, then. I'll confess first. I've been going to Boot Camp to dig up dirt on Brendan. We don't want you to marry him; he's not good enough for you. The only dirt I could find is that he's up to something with Felicity Furnleigh and Rizor Rochester. It all came to a head tonight with Rizor storming out of the gym; Brendan cancelling Boot Camp; and then a snivelling Felicity joining Brendan in his office for a quiet tête-à-tête.'

Grant stared at Fabio who's eyes were like saucers. Fifi lowered her eyes. 'While I'm still confessing, I have been coming in here every Monday night to update Fabio and Grant on any information to do with members of our leadership team. So, there. That's me all confessed. Now it's your turn and, if it helps, you can start by telling us all about Freddie Featherlow.'

Fabio choked on his drink, and Grant slapped him on his back. Amelie didn't know what to say. 'I take it that Freddie was at the gym tonight too?'

Fifi nodded. 'I couldn't work out why he wasn't losing weight, but he lifted his sweatshirt to show me the padding and pulled off his beard. I can't believe that Spacey is Lord Featherlow's estranged son!'

Amelie held her head in her hands. 'Freddie is keen to win his father's approval. He wants to be part of the family again. Chad Lagerfield tipped him off that Felicity is corrupt, and Freddie has been shadowing her to find out what she's up to. Apart from posing as Spacey, he's been sitting outside our offices dressed as a homeless man.'

Grant raised his eyebrows and Amelie continued, 'That's right. It was Freddie who told you his father was going to be abducted. That's not true – he needed a way to get you and Fabio to check the CCTV to see Felicity conspiring with him. It gave Freddie a breakthrough though when Fabio mentioned the gold bars. From the information Freddie has sourced from the gym, Felicity and Rizor are going to steal Lord Featherlow's gold bars on Christmas Eve. Brendan is lined up to do the heavy lifting.' Amelie dropped her head. 'So, we won't be getting married; it's all been one big joke.'

Fifi savoured her wine. 'Well, it sounds like everything's gone down the pan. Rizor is bound to snitch on Felicity now, and she's probably on the first flight out of the country. Goodness knows what Brendan will do. At least you won't have to spend another moment with that loser. I must admit I feel sorry for Spacey, err Freddie, though. He was crestfallen. Oh, I say, look what the cat's dragged in. Rizor's up at the bar now drowning his sorrows.'

Amelie's head was spinning. Fabio was struggling to process that his cousin was in the vicinity, and Grant had nothing but admiration for Fifi; she looked amazing after her six-week gym stint. They'd done it! One way or another, Amelie wasn't getting married to a hairless pumpkin.

'May I have a word?'

Rizor was now leaning over Fifi, staring at Fabio. Fabio stood up. 'Of course, let's find somewhere private.'

The pair stepped outside, and Rizor handed Fabio a box. 'These are stolen goods. Felicity Furnleigh is as corrupt as they come. I've been on her case for months. I've just done a deal with her. I asked her to hand over the goods and, by doing so, Featherlow Forbes would take no further action. She just needs to leave the organisation with immediate effect and take that dodgy gym manager with her. If I hadn't got to the bottom of the operation, Lord Featherlow's gold bars would have been at risk.'

Fabio looked at the box. 'Did Felicity steal these from Featherlow Forbes?'

Rizor rubbed his chin. 'I believe she colluded with a homeless person to obtain them. I want nothing to do with the whole state of affairs. I don't suggest you hand them over to the police or Featherlow Forbes will be in the press for all the wrong reasons. You're a man of substance. I'm sure you have contacts who can help you dispose of them. I'm as honest as they come; I don't want to be involved with any dodgy dealings.'

Rizor held out his hand. 'Do we have a deal?'

Fabio's eyes twinkled as he shook Rizor's hand. 'Deal.'

11

ALL IS REVEALED

Rizor headed off in the direction of the tube station with a spring in his step and Fabio walked back into the wine bar carrying the box. His colleagues waited for him in anticipation. Fabio placed the box on the table. He advised everyone on his discussion with Rizor before lifting the lid of the box.

The sparkles that darted into the dim light of the crowded room brought gasps from Fifi and Grant. Amelie sat on her hands, and Fabio's head pounded. He tried to process the events before speaking. 'How would Freddie have got hold of these?' Fabio stared at Amelie. 'They are in the same style as the collection of jewellery your friend designs. I've been studying the photographs you gave me two weeks ago. Don't tell me Freddie's corrupt too!'

Amelie shook her head. 'Freddie's the designer. The jewellery is from his collection. He used it as bait to see if Felicity took it. She did, and the rest is history. I think he's been very clever.'

Fabio gave a wry smile. 'My cousin has always been clever. There's no-one more than me that wants my uncle to welcome him back into our family. How can I get hold of him?'

Amelie smiled broadly. 'That's easy. Freddie's staying at The Fortescue Tower. I'll be delighted if you can help him.'

Fabio reached for his phone. 'Is that The Fortescue Tower? Please put me through to Freddie Featherlow's suite. What? He's checked out. That can't be possible! Oh, yes, I see. Thank you for your time.'

Everyone stared at Fabio. 'My cousin has checked out of The Fortescue Tower.'

Amelie's heart pounded. 'I have his mobile number.' Amelie called it. It went onto messaging. 'What are we going to do?'

Fabio stood up. 'I'll find a way to track my cousin down. In the meantime, I'm most concerned about Amelie. Would you like us to come back to your place? If Brendan's still there, things could get nasty.'

Amelie hadn't thought about Brendan. 'Yes, please. I don't think I can face him on my own.'

*

The door to Amelie's apartment was propped ajar by an empty tin of protein powder. Brendan's belongings had been removed, and there was no sign of a note. Amelie burst into tears. Fifi hugged her. 'Don't worry. It's for the best. I'll stay with you tonight, and then tomorrow we'll get the locks changed.'

Fabio put his arm around Amelie. 'You've been amazing throughout all of this. I won't forget it. Take the day off tomorrow and do what you have to. I'll need you back in the office after that though. You're crucial on the marketing side now that Felicity Furnleigh's done a runner.' Fabio winked, and Amelie managed a weak smile.

Grant squeezed Fifi. 'I'll stay over tonight too. I can sleep on the sofa. I can't leave all of this to you.' Fifi squeezed him back in relief. What a mess! Amelie's life had just been shattered – how was she going to cope?

*

Fabio jogged back to the office to collect his bike. When he reached the building, he checked his watch; it was nearly eleven o'clock. Lord Featherlow never went to bed before midnight. Fabio pulled out his phone. 'Uncle, it's me, Fabio. There's been a sighting of Freddie. I think I can track him down.'

Lord Featherlow's heart leapt, and his eyes welled with tears. 'Where is he? Where's my Freddie?'

'He's been staying at The Fortescue Tower, but he's just checked out. He's been trying to stop the collusion in the leadership team. Everything came to a head tonight. Felicity Furnleigh's done a runner. Rizor Rochester dobbed her in and is acting as a hero, but he's well and truly got his tail between his legs. As long as he keeps bringing in the sales, I think we should leave him in his role. We've got a gap now in marketing, Amelie's going to be crucial until we replace Felicity. It will take her mind off her wedding being cancelled.'

'Amelie's wedding's been cancelled! Wasn't that due to take place on Christmas Eve?'

'Yes, it was. But her fiancé has now left without trace. He was being lined up by Felicity to be the brawn behind her planned operation to steal your gold bars on Christmas Eve. Amelie's wedding has only ever been a decoy; the poor girl is shattered.'

Lord Featherlow couldn't help but feel a massive sense of relief. 'Great work, Fabio. With Felicity Furnleigh exposed as the rat in the pack, we can all rest in peace.'

'You can come back to work now, Uncle. I'll stand

aside as soon as you're ready.'

Lord Featherlow rubbed his forehead. 'I need you to hold the reins for a while longer. I have some family issues to sort out – starting with my wife.'

Fabio grinned. 'That's great news. Shall I continue to arrange the Featherlow Forbes Christmas Spectacular at Featherlow Manor on Christmas Eve?'

Lord Featherlow's eyes twinkled. 'I certainly think you should. And don't forget about Freddie.'

Fabio smiled down the phone. 'I won't. Leave it with me. I'll aim to return him to the family fold by Christmas.'

Lord Featherlow smiled too. 'Don't let me down, Fabio. You only have six weeks. Consider it your most important objective of the year. If you achieve that, I'll give you a bonus.'

12

BRIDGES TO BUILD

There was frost on the ground at Featherlow Manor that crisp November morning. Lord Featherlow sipped his coffee and braced himself for a trip to the dower house situated on the edge of the estate. It had been nearly five years; five years he had made excuses for the non-attendance of his wife at high society events. When Lord Featherlow had lost his son, he lost his wife too. She had moved out of Featherlow Manor and hadn't set foot inside it since. The dower house had become vacant ten years ago upon the death of Lord Featherlow's mother. It was now his wife's retreat – she'd even taken the butler with her.

The only consolation for Lord Featherlow was that Annabelle hadn't asked for a divorce. That gave him hope that one-day things would get back to normal. It had only been three months after he'd banished Freddie from the family that Lord Featherlow realised his mistake. As hard as he tried over the next few years, he couldn't find his son. There then followed the death last year of his beloved sister Foxy Forbes. Foxy had a cunning plan to tempt Freddie to re-surface, and it had worked!

Foxy had every faith that Freddie would come to his father's rescue if ever needed. She encouraged her brother to set a trap to weed out any members of the Featherlow Forbes family who were less than ethical, and things had escalated from there.

Lord Featherlow hadn't bought any gold bars; he'd made the story up and divulged it during a meeting of the leadership team. To add credence to the false statement, he boasted about increasing security at Featherlow Manor.

*

In the dower house, Annabelle was ecstatic. Freddie was home! 'Promise me you'll stay this time.'

Freddie's blue eyes twinkled. 'It depends on Father's reaction to my proposal.'

'He'll be livid when he knows you've kept in touch with me.'

'Maybe, maybe not. A lot of water's gone under the bridge since I jilted Lady Izzie Trumpton. What does Father think about Lord Trumpton being jailed for fraud?'

Annabelle smiled. 'He's delighted. The fall of Lord Trumpton just rubber-stamped your decision to extract yourself from that family.'

Freddie stared out of the window of his mother's sitting room. 'Father's walking up the drive. Does he visit you often?'

Annabelle jumped up and stood next to Freddie. 'Very rarely these days. I wonder what he's up to. I suggest you hide in the dining room. I'll deal with him.'

Freddie dashed into the next room just as the butler opened the front door. 'Good morning, Lord Featherlow.'

'Good morning, Giles, is Lady Featherlow available on this magnificent morning?'

Annabelle peered into the hallway. 'It's fine, Giles. I'll see Lord Featherlow in my sitting room. No need for refreshments.'

Lord Featherlow held his arms open wide to embrace his wife. 'Oh, Annabelle, we're getting too old now to carry on like this. I want you to come home to the manor. You can move back into the dower house when I've popped my clogs and Freddie's the next Lord Featherlow.'

Annabelle didn't move, and Lord Featherlow stepped forward to hold her in his arms. 'I received the most amazing news last night. Fabio called me from London. Freddie's been staying at The Fortescue Tower. My dearest Foxy was right. Freddie would come back to protect me at all costs. I'm pleased I lied now about those gold bars.'

Annabelle looked up at her husband. She was enjoying the feeling of being in his arms again. 'What have you done, Winston?'

'I told the leadership team I had invested in gold bars and that I'd stepped up security at Featherlow Manor. That weeded out the bad guys in the team. I'm delighted to say that our beloved son's intervention put a cat amongst the pigeons and the foulest smelling bird has taken flight. All I need now is for Fabio to track down Freddie and we can all be a family again. When Freddie comes back, I'll do anything he wants to keep him here.'

Freddie stepped into the room, and Lord Featherlow's jaw dropped. 'Anything, Father? I'm relieved to hear that. I won't ask for much.'

'Freddie! I mean it. I'll do anything it takes.'

'Allow me to marry the woman I love.'

Lord Featherlow released his wife and went over to embrace his son. 'What's her name? I'll accept her into the family whoever she is.'

Freddie coughed. 'I don't know yet. I just want a free rein to find my soulmate.'

Annabelle clasped her hands together in delight. After so many years, her family was finally reunited. She rang a small bell and Giles appeared in the doorway. 'Giles, please arrange for my things to be taken up to the manor. Normality has returned.'

Giles stifled a chuckle. 'Of course, your Ladyship. Right away!'

Lord Featherlow kept his arm around Freddie's shoulders. 'What have you been up to these last five years? I hope you've managed to have some fun.'

Freddie smiled at this father. 'I've been doing quite well for myself designing men's jewellery.'

Lord Featherlow raised his eyebrows. 'Really! We should add jewellery to the Featherlow Forbes range.'

Winston grabbed his wife's hand. 'Let's all take a stroll back to the manor. It's a brilliant day outside. I love this time of year!'

*

It was lunchtime before the re-connected family were

interrupted by visitors. Giles stepped into the dining room. 'Fabio Forbes and a lady called Amelie are waiting in the drawing room.'

Freddie's heart lurched. As far as the outside world knew, he was "missing". Lord Featherlow wiped his mouth on a serviette. 'What a surprise!' He looked at Annabelle. 'Will you please excuse me, my darling?' Annabelle nodded, and Winston winked at his son. 'I'll establish the reason for the unannounced visit. Please keep your mother entertained.'

Fabio and Amelie stood up when Lord Featherlow entered the room. Fabio was holding a box. 'We're sorry to interrupt you, Uncle, but Amelie insisted we visit you today. I'd actually given her the day off due to yesterday's debacle when her fiancé ran off with Felicity Furnleigh.'

Amelie blushed. 'That's not exactly true; we don't know if they both ran off together. All we know is that we'll never see either of them again. As far as I'm concerned, that's not a moment too soon.'

Lord Featherlow rubbed his chin; Amelie didn't look like a woman scorned. He stared at Fabio. 'What's in the box?'

Fabio opened it to the sight of sparkling jewels. 'These belong to Freddie. He used them to trap Felicity Furnleigh. Rizor Rochester retrieved them from her on the promise she wouldn't be prosecuted. You could describe it as amnesty working at its best.'

Amelie rubbed her forehead, as far as she was concerned, time was of the essence. She directed her rant at Lord Featherlow. 'The reason we are here today is that you need to realise what you've lost. You can't let a family rift go on forever. Freddie is trying his best to win your approval. However, he's now gone missing, and he could be anywhere. The sooner we find Freddie, the better!'

Annabelle and Freddie listened from the hallway. Annabelle nudged her son. 'Go on! Put Amelie out of her misery. I like her.'

Freddie walked into the drawing room, and Amelie fainted.

13

A FRESH START

Giles rushed to the kitchen to fetch the smelling salts, and Freddie carried Amelie over to the sofa. She opened her bleary eyes to the sight of his laughing ones. 'Well, I'm flattered. I've never had a woman faint at the sight of me before.'

Amelie managed a small laugh and Freddie frowned. 'This has sealed the deal for me. I expect no arguing from you. After all you have been through with your loyalty to Featherlow Forbes – even to the point of agreeing to go along with your sham of a wedding – I insist you have a week's convalescence.'

Winston raised his eyebrows at his wife, who had just entered the room. Annabelle agreed with Freddie. 'Of course, Freddie's right. You must stay with us to recover from such a terrible shock. The dower house is vacant. We'll ensure you have everything you need.'

Fabio whispered to Freddie. 'Amelie's key for me now in marketing, I need her in the office.'

Freddie shook his head. 'Now's not the time, she'll be back at work when her world's stopped spinning.'

*

Fifi phoned Grant. 'You need to come down to reception. I have some news.'

Grant flew out of the lift. 'Have you heard from Amelie?'

'Yes. She just called. She got to Featherlow Manor with Fabio, and you'll never guess what.'

'What?'

'Freddie's there.'

'So, they went all the way to the manor for nothing?'

'Not necessarily.'

'What do you mean?'

'Amelie fainted, and Freddie insisted she stays with his family for a week to convalesce. He's not taking "no" for an answer. Amelie's asked me to pack her some things and Lord Featherlow's chauffeur is coming to pick them up from reception at four o'clock.

You couldn't cover for me for an hour, could you, so that I can pop out?'

Grant smiled. 'Of course! What a turn up for the books. I can see where Freddie's coming from, Amelie's life has just imploded. A change of scenery will do her good.'

*

By six o'clock, Amelie had unpacked her suitcase in the dower house. She insisted she didn't need any staff from the manor during her stay. She was more than capable of cooking her own meals. The kitchen was fully stocked.

Amelie smiled at the sight of her cream cocktail dress and wedding shoes. Trust Fifi to pack them, although she wouldn't need them this week. Amelie intended to keep a low profile and let Freddie spend time alone with his parents. Amelie reflected on recent events; it wasn't just *her* life that had changed – Freddie's had too. Whilst Freddie was elated he was back where he belonged, Amelie's life had been brought to an abrupt halt. One minute she was planning her wedding and her future with Brendan; the next she had no idea of what lay ahead of her. Even her boss had left; that was a significant amount of change. She shuddered at the thought of the blank canvas before her.

Amelie's phone beeped with a text message:

I'M COMING OVER FOR DINNER. MY PARENTS ARE
ACTING LIKE LOVED UP TEENAGERS. IT'S
EMBARRASSING. LOVE FREDDIE X

Amelie gasped. "Love" *and* a kiss in a text message! That was very informal from the potential next Chief Executive Officer of Featherlow Forbes. What should she wear? The cocktail dress would be too much; instead, she reached for a pale pink cashmere jumper and jeans. She decided a bit of sparkle wouldn't go amiss and searched through her jewellery box that Fifi had kindly thought of packing. A pair of small diamond earrings wouldn't be too flash for a quiet dinner at home. After brushing her short sandy hair and applying another coat of mascara to accentuate her turquoise eyes, Amelie looked in the mirror and smiled at her reflection. Was it wrong to feel happy?

The doorbell rang, and Amelie ran down the stairs. Freddie stood on the doorstep with an armful of shiny green holly covered in red berries. He grinned at Amelie's surprise. 'Christmas starts here! Let's put the holly in a vase then I'll make dinner. I'll do it; these holly leaves are vicious.'

Amelie's eyes lit up. 'YOU'RE going to cook?'

Freddie held up a carrier bag. 'How does roast turkey with all the trimmings sound?'

Amelie laughed. 'That will take hours to make.'

Freddie winked. 'Not when it just needs warming up. I raided the kitchen at the manor. Mrs Baxter's been busy all afternoon making this.'

With the holly arranged in a large glass jug and placed on the kitchen table, Freddie set about turning the oven on to warm up their meals. Amelie smiled. 'You certainly know where things are in this house.'

Freddie reached for the wine glasses. 'My grandmother lived here until ten years ago; I visited her often. She enjoyed a game of Blackjack; we played for matchsticks. I think that's the biggest secret I've ever kept.'

Amelie raised her eyebrows. 'What? That your grandmother gambled?'

'No! That she smoked a pipe.'

Amelie burst out laughing, and Freddie glanced over his shoulder. 'I'm sure I could find a box of matches if you fancy a game later?'

Amelie regained her composure. 'That would be lovely. I'll look forward to that.'

Freddie poured the wine and handed a glass to Amelie. He frowned and looked deep into her eyes. 'How are you feeling, Amelie, after the shock about your wedding and everything?'

Amelie felt a calmness wash over her. 'I feel

amazing; I've had a lucky escape.'

Freddie's eyes sparkled. Amelie certainly looked amazing; he'd seen her blossom before his very eyes over a matter of weeks. He smiled at her. 'I'm relieved to hear that.'

A timer went off, and Freddie reached for the oven gloves. 'Dinner's ready! Are you OK eating in the kitchen? It's much cosier in here than the dining room.'

Amelie opened the cutlery draw. 'That will be perfect; I'll lay the table.'

With the couple seated opposite each other, Freddie raised his glass. 'Here's to you, Amelie! May the magic of Christmas bring you all the happiness you deserve.'

Amelie blushed. She was suddenly looking forward to Christmas. Freddie pushed his chair back and rushed over to the window. 'I don't believe it! It's snowing!'

Amelie stood up to join him. 'That's amazing! Wouldn't it be brilliant if it lasted until the Featherlow Forbes Christmas Spectacular on Christmas Eve?'

Freddie placed his arm around Amelie's shoulders. If the snow lasted until Christmas Eve, then there was something he must do. Freddie looked up at the tiniest of snowflakes fluttering down from the navy sky and made a wish. He turned Amelie round and stared into her beautiful eyes before leading her back to the kitchen table. 'We should eat our meal before it goes cold. Then we need to have a game of Blackjack in honour of my grandmother.'

Amelie smiled. 'Will you be smoking her pipe?'

Freddie took a mouthful of turkey then shook his head. 'I managed to slip it into her coffin when no-one was looking. It was just one of the requests she made of me. I've still got two to carry out.'

Amelie sipped her wine. 'It sounds like your grandmother was quite a character.'

Freddie gazed over Amelie's shoulder; snow was still falling outside – the flakes were getting bigger. 'Oh, she was. She certainly had a big influence on me.' Freddie turned his gaze back to Amelie before smiling. 'You could say she still does.'

14

THE HOMECOMING

The following morning, Freddie and Amelie walked down the hill from the dower house to the nearest village. Amelie gasped when she saw a name hanging from an ornate lamp post next to an arched footbridge spanning a narrow winding river. 'Featherlow Bottom! Your family has a village named after it?'

Freddie smiled. 'We own the land – it's only a small place.'

Amelie spun round to take in the sight of several small shops, a public house and a tea room. There was a church on a hill in the distance, and narrow lanes that led off the High Street to a selection of private dwellings.

'It's so cute! I love the river running through it.'

Freddie shivered and turned up the collar on his coat. His breath was visible in the cold air as he spoke. 'When we were young, Fabio and I used to go skating on the river when it froze over. Being the elder cousin, it was my idea. Aunt Foxy was none too pleased with me when we drove Fabio home soaking wet from falling over on the ice. He was never good at keeping his balance.'

Amelie laughed; she could imagine Fabio with his arms and legs flailing in contrast to Freddie skating with ease.

'Well, hello, Freddie Featherlow! What a sight for sore eyes. Are you back home for long?'

A tall, silver-haired man stood before them; Freddie's eyes lit up as he shook his hand. 'I'm back for good, Archie. Let me introduce you to Amelie; she's a friend of mine.'

Archie held out his hand to shake Amelie's. 'I'm very pleased to meet you, Amelie. Make sure Freddie brings you into the Alehouse at lunchtime. Francesca's got slow-cooked beef on the go. She'll be delighted to see young Freddie after so long.'

Archie tipped his cap and headed off in the direction of the pub. Amelie smiled when she saw the name: "Archie's Alehouse".

Freddie rubbed his gloved hands together. 'Well, that's lunch sorted. Francesca's beef is to die for.' Freddie looked at his watch. 'The problem is, it's freezing out here, and lunch isn't for another two hours.'

Freddie grabbed Amelie's hand. 'There's only one thing for it. We need to go and see Clara.'

'Who's Clara?'

'She runs the tea room over there. Clara's fruitcake is laced with rum; that'll warm us up.'

Clara squealed with delight when Freddie entered her shop. She wiped her hands on her apron and rushed over to embrace him. 'Freddie! I knew you'd be back before long. You can never keep a Featherlow away from his rightful home. What happened? Rumour has it that Lord Featherlow was none too pleased when you did a runner at the altar. If that's the case, then you send him over to me, and I'll sort things out.'

Amelie chuckled at the fire inside the tiny white-haired lady who stood before her. Her affection for Freddie was obvious.

'Clara, you are so naughty. I hope you've not been encouraging any gossip in the tea room. People would stop frequenting your premises if that was the case.'

Clara winked. 'You know the opposite's true,

Freddie Featherlow. Now, aren't you going to introduce me to your pretty young lady?'

Freddie placed a protective arm around Amelie. 'This is my friend, Amelie. She's staying with us for the week.'

Clara held the corners of her apron before curtseying. 'I'm very pleased to meet you, Amelie. You look more of Freddie's sort than the last one. Take a seat, you two. I'll bring over tea and fruitcake – it's Freddie's favourite.'

The door to the tea room flew open, and a tall, dark-haired woman rushed inside. Her shiny brown eyes scanned the room. 'Freddie! Archie told me you were home. Where have you been all this time?'

Freddie stood up, and the woman threw her arms around him. 'Hi, Francesca. Let me introduce you to Amelie. We're coming to the pub for lunch; we can catch up then. Make sure you don't overcook the beef.'

Francesca gave Freddie a playful slap on the arm and smiled at Amelie. 'He's cheeky this one. You'll have your work cut out there. I'd best get back to the kitchen; I wouldn't want to spoil my favourite boy's lunch.' Francesca winked at Amelie and blew a kiss to Freddie before turning and waving as she exited the shop.

Amelie watched Freddie savour the fruitcake.

'You're very popular, Freddie. Everyone's delighted you're back.'

Freddie blushed. 'I've known most of the tenants all my life; they're like family. Clara used to be my nanny and Francesca worked in the kitchen at the manor house before she married Archie.'

'Wow! No wonder they're so delighted to see you.'

'I'm very fond of Clara; she was the best nanny a boy could wish for. She was great friends with my grandmother and, when I grew up, my family suggested she ran the village tea room. It worked out well for her as she moved into the apartment above the shop at the same time. Everyone loves Clara.'

Amelie smiled at Clara, who was standing behind a counter watching the young couple. Clara winked and made the shape of a love heart with her arthritic hands. Amelie turned to Freddie. 'There's a real sense of community here. That's quite rare these days. It must be comforting to belong somewhere.'

Freddie reached out to take hold of Amelie's hand. His deep blue eyes bore into hers. 'It's an amazing feeling to belong somewhere. I didn't realise how much I've missed this place. Do you belong in London?'

Amelie was taken aback. 'I've never really thought about it. I've not known anywhere else.' Amelie rubbed her forehead with her free hand. 'I don't suppose I'd miss London if I found somewhere nicer to live.'

A warm feeling encompassed Freddie. In his eyes, Featherlow Bottom was the nicest place in the world.

*

After saying goodbye to Clara, the couple made their way to Archie's Alehouse. Snow crunched underfoot, and dark clouds loomed overhead. Amelie nodded towards the ornate bridge. 'Look at the robins on the bridge. There are four of them.'

Freddie glanced over. 'That'll be George, Eustace, Harold and Hector.'

'Who are they?'

'Previous Lord Featherlows. Well, that's according to my grandmother. She said there were always three robins on the bridge in winter and when grandfather died they became four.'

Amelie giggled. 'Your grandmother was funny! Look there's another one flying past. It thought of landing then took off again.'

Freddie watched the robins before opening the pub door to let Amelie walk through first. 'My grandmother was the most amazing woman. I wish you could have met her.'

*

Back at the manor, Winston had fallen off a step ladder into a heap of snow. Annabelle rushed out of the house at the sound of his screams. She hauled him onto his feet. 'I have told you before not to go up those ladders. They'll be the death of you one day. Promise me you'll act your age and ask for help next time the window needs cleaning.'

Winston's knees trembled, that had been a close shave. 'I promise, my darling. We wouldn't want five robins on the bridge in the village, would we now?'

'Your mother told you that story of hers?'

'Of course, she did. She was always trying to spook me. I never believed a word though. My mother was as nutty as one of Clara's fruitcakes!'

15

DINNER INVITATION

The next two days passed quickly for Freddie and Amelie. They'd been for long walks in the snow, followed by lunch in Archie's Alehouse, and in the evenings they cooked dinner together in the dower house. By Friday, Lord and Lady Featherlow were wondering when they were going to spend time with their son.

Annabelle smiled over the rim of her teacup. 'I have high hopes for Freddie and Amelie. He's besotted with her.'

Lord Featherlow frowned. 'But she works in marketing. She's not of the right class to marry the future Lord Featherlow.'

Annabelle glared at her husband. 'You made a promise to Freddie. He's only remained here now that you agreed to let him find a bride of his choice. If you two fall out again, I'll be requesting a divorce. Lady Izzie Trumpton was never suited to Freddie, Amelie's a much better match.'

Lord Featherlow scratched his head. 'It will take me some time to come to terms with the idea.'

His wife poured more tea. 'You *will* come to terms with it, Winston. You have to, or you'll lose me. Our son's happiness should come before your pride. Besides, Amelie appears to be a very nice young woman; we should get to know her better. I'll invite them both to dinner this evening.'

*

Amelie stared at Freddie. 'I can't go to dinner with your parents. It's very strange to get an invite. We only have two nights left – I have to leave on Sunday to get back to work.'

Freddie sensed Amelie's anxiety and stroked her hair. 'You can stay longer than Sunday.'

'No, I can't. I feel bad enough already. How am I going to explain to everyone in the office that I've spent all week with you at Featherlow Manor – well the dower house – when I should have been at work?'

Freddie felt a tinge of sadness; he hated it when reality kicked in. The last few days had been the best of his life. Amelie had a point though; they couldn't escape the outside world forever. Then the enormity of Amelie being invited to dine with his parents hit home. They had only invited Izzie to dinner once, and that was after Freddie had agreed to get engaged to her.

Freddie held Amelie's hand. 'Please come to dinner this evening. I promise my parents won't eat you alive.' Freddie winked. 'If there's any sign of them doing so, we'll leave immediately.'

Amelie cringed. She could wear her cream cocktail dress and sparkly shoes. Lord Featherlow wouldn't remember it was the same outfit she wore to the Featherlow Forbes annual party. 'All right, I'll come if it means so much to you.'

'Great! I'll drive round to collect you at seven o'clock.'

*

Freddie held his car door open for Amelie to step out. Her shoes sparkled under the floodlights that lit up the manor. She held onto his arm as they climbed the stone steps that led to the front doors. When they were inside Freddie helped her off with her coat. He felt a sudden surge of jealousy. Amelie was wearing the same cream cocktail dress she had worn to the Featherlow Forbes annual party – when Chad Lagerfield had danced with her all evening.

Lord Featherlow strode into the hall. 'Welcome! Welcome! Come through to the drawing room for an aperitif. Lady Featherlow's already on the sherry.' The couple walked into the drawing room, and Lady Featherlow stood up to embrace her son. She smiled at Amelie. 'Thank you so much for agreeing to join us for dinner, Amelie. We'll try not to bore the life out of you.'

Amelie smiled back. 'I'm sure that's not possible, Lady Featherlow.'

Lady Featherlow patted the seat beside her. 'Please call me Annabelle. I hope we can be friends.'

Freddie raised his eyebrows as Amelie sat down next to his mother. 'Now, tell me, Amelie. What's my husband like to work for? Is he an ogre in the office?'

Amelie grinned at a dismayed-looking Lord Featherlow. 'Lord Featherlow treats us all like family. He's the best boss I've ever known. We've missed him being in the office these last few weeks.'

Lord Featherlow coughed. 'You'll have a new boss at the beginning of the year. I've decided to hand over the reins to Freddie. Fabio will hold the fort for the next few weeks, but once Freddie's in place, Fabio and I will both move on.'

Annabelle narrowed her eyes at her husband. 'What will you move on to?'

'I've been meaning to buy a yacht for years. Now's the time to do it. I'll be sailing off into the sunset with you, my darling.'

Annabelle clapped her hands and Freddie felt very uncomfortable about his father's emphasis on him being Amelie's "boss". He looked over at her chatting excitedly to his mother before guiding his father to the drinks table at the other side of the room.

'I won't directly be Amelie's boss. She'll report into the new Global Head of Marketing when we've replaced Felicity Furnleigh. It's not like I'll be working closely with her on a daily basis.'

Lord Featherlow slapped his son on the back. 'You're quite right there, Freddie. Amelie will be working closely with Chad Lagerfield.'

Freddie choked on his drink. 'What??'

'Chad's been in contact with Fabio this week. He wants a move to the UK and, as his background is in marketing, it makes sense for him to replace Felicity. Chad's a good guy; I'm sure you'll agree. He's flying over on Saturday. I know you won't officially be in situ as Chief Executive Officer until January, but I think we should both go into the office on Monday to welcome Chad to his new role.'

Freddie knocked back a copious amount of wine over dinner to dull the thought of Chad working with Amelie. Lord Featherlow talked business throughout the meal to his disenchanted son, who stared across the table at his mother chatting away happily to the woman who had stolen his heart.

During the dessert course, Annabelle glanced across the table at her husband who appeared to be talking to himself; Freddie was no longer lucid. Annabelle lowered her voice. 'Lady Izzie Trumpton was never my choice for Freddie. If Winston's mother had been alive when he arranged the marriage with Lord Trumpton, she would have put a stop to it immediately. She had steadfast views on what was right for Freddie. He was her favourite grandchild. Those two were as thick as thieves.'

Amelie smiled. 'I have gathered in a very short space of time that Freddie was close to his grandmother.'

'That's an understatement. I often wondered if they could read each other's minds. In the early days, we had such large family gatherings. Foxy's family was always around; she had five children, you know – Fabio and four girls. Fabio's always been a delight, but the girls were little terrors. At one dinner there was a caterpillar on one of the girls' plates. The other three got the blame, but I saw Freddie glance over at his grandmother and chuckle when she winked back.'

'Freddie was the culprit?!'

'No, Amelie! His grandmother was. She couldn't stand those girls.'

Amelie chuckled. 'What else did they get up to?'

'When Freddie was bored at a luncheon with some stuffy business acquaintances of Winston's, his grandmother pretended to faint so that the meal ended early. I saw him walk off with a grin on his face. They were a double act those two!'

Amelie folded her serviette and placed it next to her empty dessert plate. 'How wonderful to have such a special connection with someone.'

Annabelle sighed. 'It was lovely to see, but Freddie was devastated when she died. We had an open coffin the night before her funeral and Freddie insisted on spending the last moments with her before the lid was sealed. He made us all go out of the room and said his goodbyes alone. My heart went out to him.'

Amelie looked over at a drunken Freddie having his ear chewed off by his father and suppressed a giggle at the thought of the Dowager Lady Featherlow's treasured pipe. Annabelle took in the sight of her weary son. 'I suggest Giles drives you home tonight. I've enjoyed our little chat. We must meet up again soon.'

16

A TIME FOR DANCING

Giles brought Freddie breakfast in bed on the instruction of Lady Featherlow. Freddie squinted when the curtains were drawn back to reveal a bright, crisp morning. 'I need a favour, Giles. Can you please find out where's there's dancing tonight? There must be a restaurant in a nearby town with a dinner dance going on, or a pub with live music. See what you can find and let me know.'

Half an hour later, Giles came to collect Freddie's breakfast tray. 'There are no dances planned for tonight, Sir. I've spoken to Mrs Baxter, and she said your best chance is in London. There's always dancing there.'

Freddie jumped out of bed. 'Mrs Baxter is an angel! I'll sort things from here. Amelie and I will be leaving for London this afternoon.'

Freddie called The Regenza Hotel. It was a popular venue of his father's, and with Freddie no longer needing to hide, he could go anywhere he liked. Within minutes Freddie had booked a suite and a table at this evening's Christmas Sparkle Ball. The next person he needed to speak to was his mother. Annabelle was surprised to see Freddie looking so refreshed after the amount of alcohol he had consumed the night before.

Freddie paced around his mother's sitting room. 'I have a surprise planned for Amelie. I'm taking her to the Christmas Sparkle Ball at The Regenza tonight. Any chance of borrowing one of your ballgowns? You both look the same size and height to me.'

Annabelle clapped her hands in delight. 'I have just the dress. I wore it forty years ago when your father took *me* to the ball.'

Freddie squirmed. 'I was thinking of something a bit more modern. Won't it be moth-eaten?'

Annabelle slapped Freddie on his arm. 'None of my clothes are moth-eaten. Just wait until you see it; it's perfect for Amelie.'

'OK, Mother. I trust your judgement. Will it go with the shoes she was wearing last night?'

Annabelle chuckled. 'It will go perfectly with those

gorgeous shoes. You are a funny sort, Freddie
Featherlow; any girl would be lucky to have you for a
husband.'

*

By two o'clock, Freddie and Amelie were being driven
by a chauffeur to the train station. Amelie was bursting
with excitement. 'The Christmas Sparkle Ball at The
Regenza! I never thought I would go.'

Freddie glanced sideways at her. 'I've booked a suite
for tonight too. Are you OK with that? There will be
plenty of room to avoid one another if I get drunk
again and you get cross with me.'

'That sounds perfect! I can't believe your mother
has lent me one of her dresses. When can I see it?'

'When we get to the hotel. I've not seen it either;
I've put huge faith in her judgement.'

*

By five o'clock, the couple stepped out of a black cab
at The Regenza. Amelie held her arm over her eyes at
the flashing of lights. 'What's that?'

Freddie guided her into the hotel. 'The paparazzi.
Something I've not missed while being undercover.
You'll get used to it; it comes with the territory.'

When they reached the sanctuary of the suite,

Amelie pleaded with Freddie to see the dress. He held up a large garment bag. 'Here it is. Take it to your room and don't let me see it until you're ready.'

Amelie lurched forward and kissed Freddie on the cheek. 'This is a dream come true for me. I'll go and get ready straight away.'

Freddie grinned. 'There's no rush. Let's aim to get down to the bar by seven.'

Amelie opened the door to an adjoining room, complete with its own en-suite. She placed the garment bag on the bed and unzipped it to the sight of a million sparkles. Amelie guessed it must be a million – she had never seen such a sparkly dress. She touched the teal coloured satin bodice with narrow shoulder straps and plunging neckline. However, it was the full tulle skirt embellished with crystals that made her catch her breath. If ever there was a "princess" dress, this was it.

After hanging the dress up, Amelie ran a bath and poured in the expensive bath oil from a large display of miniature toiletries. A citrus aroma filled the room and Amelie couldn't remember a time when she'd been so excited.

*

Freddie showered and changed into his dinner suit. He looked out of the window down to the hustle and bustle of London below. There wasn't much snow in

London; the pavements were covered in slush. The snow was quite deep back at Featherlow Manor. He felt nervous. What if the snow didn't last until Christmas Eve?

Freddie closed his eyes and thought back to his grandmother's words the last time they had met. He hoped now that she'd really had a vision – even if, at the time, he thought she was just talking nonsense.

Dowager Lady Featherlow had advised her grandson he would find a true princess. She said he would propose to her on Christmas Eve in the snow. She said she'd had the vision from the moment he was born when a flock of geese flew over Featherlow Manor bringing him a lifetime of luck and happiness.

Not only did his grandmother firmly believe in her vision, but she also backed it up by giving Freddie a red velvet box containing the diamond necklace and earrings her husband had given her shortly after they first met. She asked Freddie to give them to his future bride.

Freddie held the box in his hands. He had never felt inclined to give the jewellery to Lady Izzie Trumpton – but he knew now, deep in his heart, that he wanted to give it to Amelie.

The door to the adjoining room opened, and Amelie stepped through. Freddie stood up. There was no doubt in his mind that Amelie was the princess his grandmother had imagined. He stood rooted to the spot before smiling broadly. 'You look amazing!'

Amelie did a twirl, and the crystal-adorned tulle skirt swished around her. 'You don't look too bad, either! Shall we go down to the ball?'

Freddie felt the softness of the red velvet in his hands. 'I have something to give you. They were my grandmother's.' Freddie opened the box to reveal the diamond necklace and earrings.

Amelie held her hand to her chest. 'They're absolutely beautiful, but of course, I can't accept them.'

Freddie held the necklace in his hand. 'Why don't you just wear them tonight. If you want to give them back after that, then that's up to you.'

Amelie nodded, and Freddie placed the necklace around her neck before fastening the clasp. Amelie looked in a mirror as she secured the earrings in place. 'I feel like I'm dreaming, Freddie Featherlow. I'll come down with a bump in the morning.'

Freddie held out his arm for Amelie to hold onto. 'You've just come through one bump. There's no need for you to go through another. Not now that I'm here.'

17

THE CHRISTMAS SPARKLE BALL

Following a sumptuous four-course meal, the ballroom was transformed into a magical winter wonderland. Lights projected onto the walls and ceiling gave the room the appearance of a snow dome. Christmas trees sparkled, and an orchestra played hearty renditions of well-known Christmas melodies. As Freddie spun Amelie around the dancefloor, his chest was bursting with pride. He noticed several of his father's acquaintances and returned their stares with a smile.

During the evening there was a pause in the dancing for a charity auction. Amelie was delighted when Freddie bid fiercely for a cuddly polar bear with diamanté collar. Freddie gave it to Amelie, and she named it Sparkles without hesitation. Sparkles spent the next hour sitting alone on their table while Freddie and Amelie perfected their dance moves and laughed until it hurt.

At eleven o'clock, the Master of Ceremonies rang a bell. 'Ladies, gentlemen, and distinguished guests, it is now time to announce the person to be crowned this year's Miss Christmas Sparkle. I will now hand over to Mr Chad Lagerfield, the new Global Head of Marketing for Featherlow Forbes, who will present the award.'

Amelie shot a look at Freddie. 'Chad's taking over from Felicity Furnleigh?'

Freddie shrugged his shoulders. 'I only found out yesterday. He's done a deal with Fabio.'

'Why didn't you tell me? He'll be my new boss!'

'It went totally out of my mind.'

Chad Lagerfield opened a silver envelope. 'The lady to be crowned this year's Miss Christmas Sparkle is . . . Amelie Briggs.'

Amelie grabbed Freddie's knee. 'I am so embarrassed. I wouldn't have come if I'd known about this.' There was clapping around the room, and Freddie stood up to lead Amelie to the stage. He couldn't help glaring at Chad who was grinning from ear-to-ear. Amelie stepped onto the stage for Chad to place a sash over her shoulder, and a crown on her head. She had never been so humiliated in all her life. A photographer captured the scene.

After handing the crown and sash back, ready for next year's recipient, the threesome headed to Freddie and Amelie's table. Chad held out his hand to shake Freddie's. 'I'm delighted to hear you're back in the fold. It'll be great working together at Head Office.'

Chad then flashed a smile at Amelie. 'Of course, I'm looking forward to working with YOU. I've heard nothing but good reports about your performance in the marketing department.'

Amelie smiled and made an excuse to visit the Ladies cloakroom. What had just happened? She was having such a lovely time before she was dragged onto the stage. She hated being the centre of attention. Amelie caught sight of her reflection in the full-length mirror and had to look twice. She didn't think she looked like that at all. In her mind, she was still just "Amelie with the plaits".

A voice came from behind: 'I remember Annabelle wearing that dress forty years ago. She was Miss Christmas Sparkle too. She'll be delighted.'

Amelie spun round to the sight of an elderly lady in a black ballgown, with two walking sticks. 'You know Lady Featherlow?'

'You could say that I was acquainted with the Dowager Lady Featherlow. She was a great woman.'

Amelie reached out to help the old lady to a chair. 'Oh, there's no need for that, dear. It was a pleasure to meet you. It'll soon be Christmas.'

The old lady turned round, and Amelie looked back at her reflection in the mirror. She wasn't just plain old Amelie Briggs anymore. Since meeting Freddie, she had changed. Amelie realised that not every day would be magical, but Freddie was bringing out the best in her. Trust him to forget to tell her about Chad Lagerfield – he'd been more interested in bringing her to London and giving her the night of her life.

Amelie touched up her make-up then headed back into the ballroom. There was still time for dancing! She was surprised to find Freddie sitting alone with Sparkles on his lap. Amelie sat next to him. 'Where's Chad gone?'

'He's doing me a favour. Lady Izzie Trumpton's mother just marched over and made it clear I'm still in her bad books. I swear she'd have hit me with her handbag if Chad hadn't charmed her round. He's dancing with her over there.'

Amelie saw Chad dancing with a tall, silver-haired lady, who was dressed in midnight blue velvet and dripping with sapphires. 'Oh, dear. It could have been worse; Lady Izzie may have been at the ball tonight herself.'

Freddie glanced sideways at Amelie. 'She is – that's the problem. She noticed you're wearing Grandmother's jewels.'

'How does she know they're your grandmother's jewels?'

'Because my father has a log of everything he keeps in the family vault. I caught Izzie in his study one day reading the folder he had left on his desk.'

'What did you do?'

'I was about to break things off with her there and then. But my father marched past me and took the folder from her. He tried to make light of the matter by showing her a photograph of the necklace and earrings you are wearing tonight. He told her that one day they would be hers.'

'Why would he do that?'

'Because my grandmother wanted me to give the jewels to my future wife.'

Amelie touched the diamond necklace around her neck. 'No wonder Lady Izzie's upset.'

Freddie jerked Amelie towards him just in time to see the drink that was aimed at her fall to the floor.

Amelie gasped at the sight of a tall, willowy blonde standing over her, holding an empty champagne flute. 'Too right, I'm upset. Have YOU ever been jilted? Have YOU suffered humiliation?'

Amelie stood up, taking care to avoid the wet patch on the floor. 'I have suffered humiliation, but I have risen above it.'

Freddie placed Sparkles on the table and glared at Izzie. 'A lady should act with decorum, not in the way in which you have just humiliated yourself.' He could have said more but chose to keep his dignity.

Izzie's red face clashed with her scarlet dress before she stormed off to extract her mother from Chad's embrace. 'We need to leave now Mother!'

Freddie held Amelie in his arms and spun her around the dancefloor. 'Have I ever told you that you're amazing?'

Amelie giggled. 'What you didn't tell me was that your mother was crowned Miss Christmas Sparkle in this very dress forty years ago.'

Freddie held Amelie at arm's length to look at her. 'Was she?!'

'You didn't know?'

'How could I? I wasn't born. How did *you* find out?'

'An old lady in the cloakroom mentioned it.'

'Was she a friend of Mother's?'

Amelie shook her head. 'She said she was "acquainted with the Dowager Lady Featherlow".'

'But my grandmother's dead. I thought all her friends were too. What did she look like?'

Amelie could picture the lady perfectly. 'She was quite small and walked with the aid of two sticks. She wore a black ballgown. She said that the Dowager Lady Featherlow was a "great woman".'

Freddie's heart pounded. 'Did she say anything else?'

'Come to mention it, she did. She said it had been a pleasure to meet me and that "it'll soon be Christmas". I thought that was a bit strange, but everyone's looking forward to Christmas, aren't they?'

Freddie held Amelie close. He could picture the Featherlow Forbes Christmas Spectacular at Featherlow Manor on Christmas Eve and knew now, for sure, that snow would be on the ground. His earlier wish had been granted – his grandmother approved of Amelie. He was certain the Dowager Lady Featherlow would do everything in her power to make her vision, and his dreams, come true.

18

THE SUNDAY PAPERS

At Featherlow Manor, Lord and Lady Featherlow were taking breakfast in the morning room. Annabelle had missed the bright blue and yellow decorated room during her stay in the dower house. 'I do so love the view from this room, Winston. The ornamental gardens look so pretty in the snow.'

'They look magnificent all year round, my darling.'

Giles entered the room with the Sunday papers. He'd had a quick look at the headlines and left them folded on the appropriate pages. Annabelle knew when Giles was up to mischief. 'You have a twinkle in your eye, Giles. Why have you folded the papers differently this morning?'

Giles blushed. 'I remember when you wore that dress, your Ladyship. You were the talk of the town that Christmas.'

Giles exited the room, and Winston and Annabelle grabbed the papers. Annabelle squealed with delight. 'Amelie won! I knew she would. Freddie will be thrilled.'

Winston rubbed his chin. 'I fear that I am grossly outnumbered in my concern over this union.'

Annabelle scanned the photographs. 'Yes, you are. Even your mother approves.'

'My mother's been dead for ten years.'

'She'll still be keeping an eye on Freddie. You know how close those two were.'

'How do you know she approves?'

'She gave me a drawing when Freddie was born.'

'A drawing? Who drew it?'

'Your mother did. She was quite an artist; Freddie takes after her.'

'What was the drawing of?'

'Freddie proposing to Amelie in the snow on Christmas Eve.'

Winston nearly choked on his croissant. 'What a load of old tosh!'

Annabelle sipped her tea. 'I knew what your reaction would be. That's why I've not told you about it before.'

'Does Freddie know about this?'

'No. Your mother asked me to keep the drawing until the deal was done and then to give it to Freddie as an engagement present from her.'

Winston shuffled in his seat. 'But Freddie was going to get married on Christmas Eve, five years ago, to Lady Izzie Trumpton. Didn't you wonder then that my mother had got things wrong?'

Annabelle shook her head. 'I always knew that Freddie wouldn't go through with it.'

'But I spent a fortune on that outfit for you!'

'I know, dear. If you had listened to my concerns at the start, then you wouldn't have needed to. Of course, I'll need a different outfit for the real wedding.'

Winston laughed. 'I think my mother was away with the fairies and you are taking after her.'

Annabelle stood up and stormed out of the room; she returned with the drawing. Winston surveyed his mother's artwork from all angles – there was no denying that the girl with Freddie was an exact likeness to Amelie.

Winston's blood ran cold. 'Was my mother a witch?'

Annabelle clasped his hand. 'Your mother was an extremely talented woman. It brings me great comfort, knowing that Freddie has finally found true happiness.'

*

In central London, shoppers bustled throughout the crowded streets, and Christmas trees twinkled in the dull afternoon light. There was a sense of anticipation before London's spectacular Christmas illuminations sprang into life for the evening. Grant bought a bag of roasted chestnuts from a street vendor, and Fifi smiled up at him with her baby blue eyes before tucking in. Grant grinned as he divulged his surprise to her. 'I've bought some tickets for an event.'

Fifi tightened her woollen scarf around her neck and rubbed her gloved hands together. She wished she'd worn her bobble hat; icy wind whipped past her ears, and her feet were freezing due to her suede boots soaking up slush from the perilous pavements. Fifi would rather be anywhere else than outside braving the wintry chill in the middle of November. She looked up at Grant. 'What event?'

'Ice-skating.'

'Who are we going to watch?'

'We're not watching. We're doing it.'

Fifi cringed as Grant gestured to a queue over the road. 'We should head over; we wouldn't want to miss our place.'

Grant wasn't surprised that Fifi was unusually quiet. He smiled at her. 'Are you sure you want to give this a go? It took me a while to get to grips with it, and I was just a fearless toddler at the time. You won't get jealous watching me perform a few Axel jumps, will you? I'm also a master of backspins; I'll try to teach you those for starters – that's if you really want to give this a go.'

Fifi felt sick. She really didn't want to go ice-skating, she had less padding now that she'd lost a stone. She'd have to go through with it though, or Grant would think she was a coward; there was no way she would let that happen.

There were only eight people in front, and Fifi's heart was pounding. Grant wondered how much longer she would hold out before she "ducked out" of the queue; he loved winding her up. There were two tall women behind them wearing fur hats. 'Don't worry, Sis. I'll find the dirt on this Amelie Briggs. How could she humiliate you like that at The Regenza of all places? Her ugly face is splattered all over the Sunday papers. We'll find a way to drag her down to the gutter where she belongs.'

Fifi and Grant stared at each other before edging their way out of the queue. Fifi couldn't resist turning round to glare at the evil women. As she did so, her eyes were drawn to a Mulberry bag. There was a booking confirmation slip peeking out of the top – Fifi saw the name: "Trumpton".

The couple headed for the nearest newspaper stand. They bought copies of the Sunday papers and found a table inside a small coffee shop. With Fifi's mouth wide open, Grant did the talking. 'Amelie was at The Regenza last night with Freddie Featherlow. She won the Miss Christmas Sparkle title. Doesn't she look amazing?!'

Fifi concentrated on the "write up" of proceedings before staring at Grant. 'You should have recognised her. You've worked for Featherlow Forbes longer than Amelie and me.'

'Who?'

'The tall blonde in the fur hat.'

'Why?'

'It says here that "Lady Izzie Trumpton was jilted by Freddie Featherlow on Christmas Eve five years ago".'

Grant grabbed hold of the newspaper. 'Let me see. Oh, yes! I remember her now. She doesn't look too good in that last shot. A "face of thunder" doesn't even cover it.'

'She's out to get Amelie! What are we going to do?'

Grant sipped his nutmeg and orange Christmas coffee; it tasted good. No-one had been more relieved than him when Freddie had jilted Lady Izzie Trumpton at the altar. She'd been a frequent visitor to Head Office and always insisted on using Lord Featherlow's office. He'd caught her on more than one occasion rummaging through the desk drawers. She'd threatened to get him the sack if he ever snitched on her. Maybe now was payback time.

Fifi raised her voice. 'Grant! This is serious. Are you listening to me?'

Grant licked his lips. 'Amazing coffee. Yes, I am listening to you, Fifi, and I know exactly what to do.'

'What?'

'We put Lady Izzie Trumpton in touch with Rizor Rochester. They're both as corrupt as they come. When they try to bring Amelie down, we'll catch them both in the act. It will be a classic case of "killing two birds with one stone".'

'Can we really do that?'

'Of course.' Grant reached over and squeezed Fifi's hand. 'All you need to do is trust me. I'm on the case.'

Fifi bit into a cinnamon doughnut, then wiped her mouth on the back of her hand. 'Well, make it quick, Grant McGuire. Otherwise, I'll put that stone back on.'

Grant winked. 'I'll have it sorted by Christmas.'

Fifi grinned. 'If you get it sorted by Christmas you'll be my hero.'

Grant chuckled. 'It's a deal!'

19

BACK IN THE OFFICE

Monday morning and Chad Lagerfield's priority was Amelie. 'I've booked a meeting room for today; I need you to update me on what's been going on in Marketing. Don't worry about divulging Felicity Furnleigh's misdemeanours. If I don't know what she was planning, I won't be able to steer the boat into safer waters.'

Amelie walked into the room behind Chad. 'Do you sail?' She then blushed, of course "Action Man" sailed, what a silly question.

Chad closed the meeting room door and his eyes twinkled. 'I do.'

Amelie continued to blush. 'Felicity didn't confide in me. I can show you the monthly reports and how to navigate the IT system but, apart from that, I just did my job.' Amelie sighed. 'I wasn't encouraged to do anything else.'

The door to the meeting room flew open, and Lord Featherlow entered. 'Welcome to the UK, Chad! Did you have a good flight over on Saturday? Pretty impressive that you managed to get to The Regenza in time to present the Miss Christmas Sparkle award.'

Chad smiled at Amelie. 'It was my pleasure.'

Lord Featherlow coughed. 'Indeed. Well done, Amelie. My wife's dress suited you.'

Freddie appeared from behind his father. 'Amelie would have won whatever dress she was wearing. I'll need to find another occasion for her to wear Grandmother's jewels. They're yours now Amelie; I've only agreed to put them back in the vault at Featherlow Manor for safekeeping.'

Amelie shook her head. 'You know I can't accept them.'

Grant was hovering outside the meeting room. He saw Rizor Rochester at the drinks machine and went over to grab a coffee. 'They're talking about Saturday night's ball at The Regenza in there. Amelie was thrilled to wear the Dowager Lady Featherlow's diamond necklace and earrings. They're worth a fortune. It's a good job Freddie's arranged for them to be put back in the vault at Featherlow Manor.'

Rizor's eyes widened, and Grant continued, 'Mind you, Lord Featherlow's been a bit lapse with leaving his security codes on his desk. Freddie advised me his former fiancée, Lady Izzie Trumpton, has access to information that could cause the Lord huge problems. I'm surprised she hasn't used it yet.'

Rizor had turned a new leaf. A couple of weeks back he'd have been interested in that snippet of information. Instead, he decided to park it in the corrupt part of his brain that he was struggling to keep shut.

Lord Featherlow called over to the Global Head of Sales. 'Rizor! We're convening in ten minutes. We'll use the boardroom.'

Rizor waved to signal he'd got the message and Grant continued with his plan. 'Freddie's going to the wine bar at six o'clock. It would be good for you two to become acquainted.'

Rizor scratched his head. 'Thanks for the tip-off. I was going anyway.' Rizor slapped Grant on the back and headed to the boardroom.

Grant was thinking quick; he was impressed he could pull together a cunning plan at a moment's notice. He walked over to Rizor's desk and picked up a sheet of personalised headed paper. He then sat down at his own desk, typed a note, put the headed paper in a printer and picked up the phone to call the chauffeur.

Forty minutes later, the chauffeur knocked on the door of Lady Izzie Trumpton's west London townhouse. He gave an envelope to the butler, who presented it to Lady Izzie on a silver tray. She turned it over and was surprised to see the Featherlow Forbes logo embossed on the back. Izzie unfolded the letter and ran her finger over Rizor Rochester's signature. She was intrigued. Why would the Global Head of Sales of her ex-fiancé's organisation want to meet her in a wine bar at six o'clock this evening?

*

Back in the office, Fabio outlined his proposals for the Featherlow Forbes Christmas Spectacular. 'We only have five weeks to turn around what will be Featherlow Forbes' most exclusive customer event in history. Invitations to Featherlow Manor on Christmas Eve will be as scarce as the golden tickets in Willy Wonka's chocolate bars.'

Freddie chuckled. 'I hope I get an invite.'

Fabio grinned. 'You're one of the stars of the show!' Freddie raised an eyebrow and Fabio continued, 'I thought it would be a hoot if the Featherlow Forbes leadership team modelled next season's collection.'

There were shrieks of laughter and cries of: 'No way!' around the boardroom.

Lord Featherlow rubbed his chin. 'Fabio has a point. It would be good to prove we practise what we preach; attending the event in Featherlow Forbes attire should be a given for everyone in this room.'

Rizor glanced around at the horrified faces. 'But we're all different shapes and sizes – and ages. It's a big ask to get us all to strut our stuff in front of our major customers. We'll end up being a laughing stock.'

Lord Featherlow slapped a hand on the table. 'Fabio's idea is approved. Everyone looks good in Featherlow Forbes clothing.'

Chad's marketing brain kicked in. 'We could unveil a new slogan: *Featherlow Forbes from Father to Son*.'

Lord Featherlow looked at Fabio. 'How would you feel about that? Do you think my dearest Foxy would approve?'

Fabio grinned. 'She'd love it! I think it's a great idea. It'll appeal to all generations – we need to increase our younger customer base. With the addition of Freddie's jewellery collection, we'll be reaching out to a whole new audience.'

Rizor sat back in his chair and twiddled his thumbs. He could imagine the sales flooding in; his bonuses would go through the roof. 'When are we going to have an official sighting of the jewellery?'

Fabio gazed at Grant through the glass wall of the boardroom. Grant stuck his thumb in the air; that meant the wine bar "date" was on for six o'clock. If there was one job Fabio wanted to do before he moved on at the end of the year, that was to get rid of Rizor Rochester – once a thief, always a thief.

Fabio turned his gaze to Rizor. 'We need to keep this information within these four walls; the jewellery collection we'll be launching on Christmas Eve is worth millions. Freddie's sourced the best diamonds from South Africa, exquisite emeralds from Columbia and spectacular sapphires from Ceylon.'

Rizor rubbed his hands together. 'What about rubies?'

Fabio kept a straight face. 'Myanmar is the place to go for rubies. You could say that Freddie's left no stone unturned in his quest for the best.'

Freddie suppressed a chuckle, and Lord Featherlow squirmed in his chair. Fabio watched Rizor's eyes flicker at the prospect of coming into contact with a potential fortune – a fortune Rizor considered the buffoons he worked with were ill-equipped to protect. Fabio continued to dangle bait in front of Rizor, who was dribbling in anticipation.

Fabio frowned. 'We need to keep the location of the jewellery secret. It won't be moved to the vault at Featherlow Manor until Christmas Eve. Freddie will give us all a sneak peek at the Christmas Spectacular. It will be the highlight of the event.'

Lord Featherlow wondered what on earth Fabio was playing at. He felt extremely uncomfortable. His nephew could be quite the clown at times; it would be a relief when Freddie took over. 'Well, I suggest we call it a day for now. I'm heading back to the manor, can I give you a lift, Freddie?'

Fabio glared at his cousin. 'Freddie's staying in town tonight. We're going for a drink in the wine bar at six o'clock.'

Lord Featherlow nodded. 'So be it. Good work with the preparations for the event on Christmas Eve, Fabio. I'll leave everything in your capable hands.' Lord Featherlow hid a grimace; nothing could be further from the truth – he needed to get Fabio some help.

The leadership team exited the boardroom, except for Fabio and Freddie. Fabio signalled to Grant to join them. Freddie laughed. 'What was that all about?'

Fabio frowned. 'I'll let Grant update you.'

Grant paced around the room in line with his spinning thoughts. 'Lady Izzie Trumpton is out to get Amelie. It's a classic case of "a woman scorned".

Anyway, I decided to devise an evil plan and find a way of getting her to take ownership of it.'

Freddie raised his arms in the air. 'So, that's what Fabio's performance was about just now. I'm afraid you need to fill me in with more details.'

Grant continued, 'When you were engaged to Lady Izzie, she kept coming into the office and rummaging through your father's desk drawers. Fabio told me you caught her looking at private papers on Lord Featherlow's desk at the manor. Is there a chance she will have seen the vault security code?'

Freddie nodded. 'She definitely saw the code. My father was convinced she would soon be part of our family, so he wasn't bothered. I told my mother, and she had the code changed.'

Grant punched the air. 'That's great news. My plan can go ahead without any risk.'

Freddie was intrigued. 'What's your plan?'

'I've invited Lady Izzie to meet Rizor Rochester in the wine bar at six o'clock this evening. Once those two get talking, they are bound to concoct a plan to break into the vault at Featherlow Manor. Don't forget that Rizor still believes Lord Featherlow has invested in gold bars.'

Freddie winked at his cousin. 'And with Fabio's

help, he now thinks my jewellery range is worth a small fortune. They'll plan the heist for Christmas Eve when they believe the collection will be there. Good work, Grant!'

Grant chewed his bottom lip. 'The only thing we can't be certain about is how Lady Izzie is going to "get Amelie".'

Freddie stood up and held Grant's shoulders. 'What exactly have you heard?'

'I heard something about "dragging her down to the gutter where she belongs".'

Freddie's heart sank. 'Amelie mustn't hear a word about this. We'll need to protect her; I don't want her left alone for a moment.'

Grant nodded. 'Fifi's aware of what's going on. She'll help us; she'd do anything for Amelie. You or Amelie shouldn't turn up at the wine bar tonight. I'll go with Fabio and Fifi. I need to get Rizor and Izzie connected when they turn up. Things will fall into place after that.'

Freddie reached for his phone. 'I'll book a suite at The Fortescue Tower again to use while I'm in London. I'll take Amelie out for dinner.'

20

A PLAN IN PROGRESS

Rizor entered the wine bar at five forty-five. He looked for Freddie, who had left the office five minutes earlier. Grant jumped up from the stool he was sitting on and headed to the bar. Fifi and Fabio stared at each other and tried to listen to what Grant had to say. Fifi crossed her fingers and prayed that he could pull this off.

'Oh, hi, Rizor.'

'Where's Freddie?'

'He couldn't make it. He's rushed off to a business meeting.'

Rizor turned round to exit the building when Lady Izzie walked in. Grant gulped; he'd never viewed himself as a master of ad-lib; he was in at the deep end now. 'Lady Izzie, how nice to see you. Have you met our Global Head of Sales, Rizor Rochester?'

Izzie was irritated that Lord Featherlow's annoying Executive Assistant was invading her personal space. She winked at Rizor and glared at Grant before sashaying into the Ladies cloakroom. She was sure Rizor Rochester would get rid of the unwanted hanger-on before she returned.

Grant grinned at Rizor. 'She winked at you!'

Rizor frowned. 'Who is she?'

'Lady Izzie Trumpton; the woman I told you about earlier. Good job Freddie had to go to a business meeting tonight, there's no love lost between those two.' Grant nudged Rizor. 'I think you're in there, mate. She's worth a small fortune.'

Grant returned to his seat, and Rizor ordered a bottle of champagne, and two glasses. Izzie returned from her self-enforced interlude and headed straight for Rizor. 'Champagne! My favourite.'

Rizor handed her a glass. 'I'm very pleased to meet you, Lady Izzie. I hear you are familiar with the Featherlow Forbes family.'

Izzie sniffed. 'For my sins. I'm looking forward to sharing information with you, in return, I want dirt on

Amelie Briggs.'

Rizor raised his eyebrows. 'Why would you be interested in one of our marketing assistants? I have much more interesting information I could divulge to you – I'm not on the leadership team for nothing.'

Izzie huffed. She'd hear what Rizor had to say then use his divulgences to bring Amelie down.

Fifi edged along the bar with her back to Izzie and Rizor. Izzie was whispering. 'So, you're telling me you nearly broke into the vault before, but you bottled it and snitched on your accomplices?'

Rizor kept his voice low. 'I wasn't working with a crack team that time, and you've just told me you have access to one. You also know the code to the vault.'

'I have access to everyone. My father has contacts.'

'Are we on then for Christmas Eve?'

Izzie held out her soft, manicured hand. 'Let's shake on it.'

Fifi edged away, then hurried over to join Fabio and Grant. She held up her hand to high-five them both. 'Grant's a genius. The heist is on for Christmas Eve.'

*

Lord Featherlow sat opposite his wife at the dining

table. 'I'm worried Fabio is going to fall flat on his face with the Featherlow Forbes Christmas Spectacular. His heart's in the right place, but I fear he has no idea his capabilities are lacking in certain areas. Our nephew lives in cloud cuckoo land; you should have heard what he came out with today at the leadership team meeting. I had to cut it short before he spurted out more of his fantasy world nonsense. I'm trying to run a business here; not a kindergarten.'

Annabelle placed her knife and fork down; she hated seeing her husband so agitated. 'Why don't I help out? The Christmas Spectacular is going to be held here at the manor. Why can't I work with Fabio to ensure things run smoothly?'

His wife's offer touched Winston. 'Do you know, I might take you up on that. It's the administration side that will still be an issue. You can't possibly take that on. We need to get timely invitations out to our top customers – Fabio should have done that weeks ago. There will need to be gifts for the ladies; enough catalogues for people to take away; maybe a raffle or something to add a bit of interest.' Winston sighed. 'The list's endless. Fabio won't think of half of the things that need doing.'

Annabelle shuddered. 'Oh, I see. No wonder you're concerned. Who's idea was this anyway?'

Winston looked at his wife. 'Amelie's.'

Annabelle was thrilled. 'I have a solution to all of your problems then. I can either base myself in London until Christmas Eve, or Amelie comes back down here and stays in the dower house. We can do all the intricate work, and Fabio can front it. He's a good frontman – such a charmer.'

Winston never ceased to be amazed at how his wife always got her way. 'It would make sense if you both work from here, my darling. The manor needs to look its best. Make sure there are plenty of Christmas trees – and lights. Don't forget the lights.'

Annabelle smiled. 'I won't. I feel quite excited to be working with Amelie and Fabio. I'll start to make a list.'

*

Freddie's phone was on silent in the restaurant. It wasn't until the couple stepped outside onto the slush-covered pavement that he noticed four missed calls from his father. Freddie called him back.

Lord Featherlow sounded jovial. 'Your mother has had a brainwave. I advised her of my concern over Fabio's capability at organising the Christmas Spectacular, and she has offered to step in to manage the intricate side of things. She's always been a stickler for detail. Anyway, it would make sense if Amelie moved back to the dower house to help her. It's too big a job for your mother to do on her own.'

Freddie's eyes lit up. 'What a brilliant idea! After Fabio's performance at the meeting today, I was beginning to wonder how he would cope with such a complex task. What does Chad think about losing Amelie?'

'I haven't told him yet. He can get a temp in until Christmas. Amelie will only be at the other end of the phone if he needs her advice.'

Freddie winked at an inquisitive Amelie. 'I'll come back home with Amelie tomorrow. Goodnight, Father. See you soon.'

Amelie had managed to piece together the majority of the conversation. 'Do I get a say in this?'

Freddie hugged her. 'No.'

'What about your suite at The Fortescue Tower?'

'I'll keep it booked for now. We may want to pop back at weekends to do some dancing.'

Amelie blushed. 'That's far too extravagant, Freddie Featherlow.'

Freddie grinned. 'You're right. I'll let Grant and Fifi use it when we're away.'

'Grant and Fifi?!!'

'Yes. It's about time they admitted how crazy they

are about each other.'

'I didn't know that!'

'Neither do they. They'll realise soon enough. Love will find a way – it always does.'

21

TIME FOR A DAY OFF

Two weeks later calm ensued at Featherlow Manor. Giles walked into the morning room with afternoon tea for Annabelle and Amelie. Annabelle leant back in her chair. 'What a whirlwind the last two weeks have been, but we're on track now, Amelie. I'm so pleased we chose to use this room as our office. It's far too sunny and bright to only use for an hour in the mornings.'

Amelie wandered over to the French windows. Snowflakes were fluttering around outside; and the delivery of twelve ten-foot-tall Christmas trees was being offloaded behind the strategically-placed trellis that hid the vegetable garden from view of the manor. Amelie turned round. 'The trees are here! The gardeners will be able to give them a good watering before the decorators arrive on Friday.'

'Perfect! Now we know the exact numbers for the event we can firm up on the catering and ensure we have enough gifts for the ladies. Are we in agreement we're going for the silver snow domes?'

'I think so. They're so unusual. When they're unboxed each Christmas, the recipients will think of Featherlow Forbes. It's a good marketing ploy.'

'You're so right; snow domes it is!' Annabelle laughed. 'I'm having so much fun working with you, Amelie. We could run our own business.'

Amelie giggled. 'Maybe we shouldn't advertise our Events Management talents yet. We need to see if the Featherlow Forbes Christmas Spectacular goes without a hitch.'

Annabelle bit into a cucumber sandwich before wiping her mouth on a serviette. 'I've just thought of something else we need to do.'

Amelie studied her lengthy list of tasks and wondered what they'd missed. 'What's that?'

'We need to get you a pretty dress. You can't keep borrowing mine. I've seen one in Cherry Conti's boutique; I can picture you wearing it.'

Amelie laughed. 'There's no need. I've got that cream cocktail dress and my sparkly shoes. Besides,

Cherry Conti dresses cost a fortune.'

Annabelle shook her head and held her hand up to silence Amelie's protest. Cherry is an old friend of mine. 'I absolutely insist that you wear the dress I have found for you. It needs to be that one. We can take a well-deserved day off tomorrow and pop into London.'

*

Lord Featherlow was delighted things were progressing well with the Featherlow Forbes Christmas Spectacular. He could always rely on his wife to save the day. He still felt unnerved about his mother predicting Freddie proposing to Amelie – it all seemed very odd. Surely he would have known if his mother was an artist. Winston certainly remembered Annabelle drawing a very lifelike picture of him when they first met. His eyes twinkled . . . now why didn't he think of that before?

*

On the train into London, Amelie was unusually quiet. Annabelle glanced sideways at her. 'Are you annoyed with me?'

Amelie looked directly at Lady Featherlow. 'Yes, I am. I don't want you to buy me a dress from Cherry Conti's. I feel you are doing it for you rather than me.'

Annabelle held her head in her hands. 'I've been very naughty, and Winston is going to kill me.'

Amelie laughed. 'Surely, whatever you've done doesn't warrant Lord Featherlow committing murder?'

Annabelle reached into her folio case and produced the drawing of Freddie and Amelie. 'I've scared the life out of Winston when all I wanted was to make him see sense – with a little help from his mother.'

Amelie's eyes widened. 'Freddie gets his artistic nature from you!'

'Yes, he does. It's Winston's fault in a way that he doesn't remember I drew a portrait of him when we first met. I took an opportunity, and I'm afraid it's going to backfire miserably.'

'Please tell me more.'

'Winston always listened to his mother, so I told him she'd had a vision of Freddie proposing to you on Christmas Eve and had given me the drawing to give to Freddie as a present from her when the deal was done.'

Amelie's mouth fell open. 'What did Lord Featherlow say about that?'

'Not a lot. He's spooked. He thinks his mother was a witch. If we don't buy that dress from Cherry Conti's I'm afraid all my hopes and dreams will be shattered.'

Amelie touched Annabelle's arm. 'Here's what we're going to do. We will have a lovely time in London today. We can even go to Cherry Conti's, and I'll try the dress on. There's no way we're buying it though. When we get back to the manor tonight, you need to put Lord Featherlow out of his misery and own up to what you've done. You'll feel much better after that.'

'Do you think so?'

'I know so. We won't have had a wasted trip as I need to pick up Sparkles from my apartment. I forgot to pack him in all the rush with everything, but I couldn't bear to be without him as we get nearer to Christmas. Freddie outbid everyone at the Christmas Sparkle Ball auction – Sparkles will always be special to me.'

'Is Sparkles a puppy?'

Amelie chuckled. 'No! He's a polar bear. You'll love him when you meet him.'

*

Following a quick stop at Amelie's apartment, the couple headed to Cherry Conti's. Annabelle stroked the polar bear poking out of Amelie's bag. 'Freddie's a sentimental old fool; he takes after his father. I hope I haven't ruined everything with Winston.'

'That's never going to happen. Lord Featherlow will

be so pleased when you own up about the drawing; it's not nice to let him think that his mother was a witch.'

Both women laughed. 'You're good for me, Amelie. I always wanted a daughter.'

Amelie left her bag with Annabelle while she tried on the dress. Annabelle sipped champagne and chatted to Cherry Conti's staff who knew her well; she didn't notice the tall girl in a fur hat surveying Amelie's bag.

Lady Sophie Trumpton slipped off her diamond bracelet and attached it to Sparkles' diamante collar. She went into a changing room and messaged her sister:

> I'VE PLANTED MY BRACELET ON AMELIE BRIGGS.
> WELL, ON HER STUPID SOFT TOY TO BE PRECISE.
> COULDN'T BELIEVE MY LUCK WHEN SHE TURNED
> UP AT CHERRY CONTI'S. WE CAN GET HER
> ARRESTED FOR THEFT. WHAT SHALL I DO NEXT?

Amelie stepped into the room in a cloud of turquoise chiffon. Annabelle handed her champagne flute to a member of staff and walked over to hug her. 'Please let me buy this for you.'

Amelie shook her head. 'We have a deal. No dress for me and no more worry for Lord Featherlow about his mother.'

Annabelle sighed. 'If you insist. Once you're changed we'll head over to Tower Bridge, and I'll buy you lunch at one of my favourite restaurants.'

Lady Izzie messaged her sister back:

WAIT UNTIL SHE LEAVES CHERRY CONTI'S.
THEN FOLLOW HER. I'M ON MY WAY.

Annabelle and Amelie stepped out of a black cab at Tower Bridge. They were about to enter the restaurant when two chauffeur-driven cars pulled up outside. Lady Sophie flew out of the first car. 'Stop that woman! She's stolen my bracelet. Call the police!' She pointed a well-manicured fingernail at Amelie's bag. 'There it is, she's attached it to her stuffed toy.'

Lady Izzie climbed out of the second car. 'The police are on their way. How dare Amelie Briggs steal from the Trumpton family? We'll have her locked up. The reputation of Miss Christmas Sparkle is now in tatters. It's about time she got her comeuppance.'

A police car pulled up behind the limousines. Two officers emerged, and Annabelle waved them over. 'Good afternoon, Officers. I am well acquainted with the Trumpton sisters. They are not averse to playing games and having a bit of fun.'

Lady Izzie glared at Annabelle and spat her words out: 'Amelie Briggs is a thief!'

Annabelle shook her head and smiled at the officers. 'The only people who should be arrested are these two young women. We could arrange for them to be charged with defamation of character and wasting police time.'

The officers looked at one another, and Annabelle handed one of them her phone. 'I recorded the whole charade on here. I am also aware there were CCTV cameras in the room where Lady Sophie Trumpton decided to play a little game and plant her bracelet in Amelie's handbag.'

Lady Sophie's jaw dropped to the floor, and her sister spoke on her behalf. 'We won't be taking this any further; it was an accident. Sophie's bracelet must have a faulty catch.'

Annabelle took her phone back from the officer, and Amelie held Sparkles aloft for Lady Sophie to retrieve her bracelet. She was careful not to get her fingerprints on the offending item. The Trumpton sisters climbed into their cars, and Annabelle turned to the police officers. 'We're so sorry for wasting your time, Officers. You know what young girls are like, always up to a prank or two. Now please excuse us, or we'll be late for our luncheon appointment.'

22

THE AFTERMATH

Annabelle ordered a gin and tonic and downed it in two. 'That was a close shave.'

Amelie's face was white, and she held her trembling hands in her lap. 'What do you mean?'

'I left your bag unattended while I drank champagne and chatted to the staff.'

'Do you mean you didn't record the incident?'

'Of course, I didn't record it. If I'd seen it happen, I'd have stopped the evil woman in her tracks. Those Trumpton girls won't be raising their ugly heads for quite some time now. Thank goodness.'

*

Izzie was livid with her sister. 'You are such a stupid

waste of space! You do realise what you've just done, don't you?' Sophie shook her head. 'You've put us both in the limelight when we should be undercover. We've lost any chance of framing that pathetic Amelie Briggs now. We need to cut our losses and move on.'

Sophie's eyes widened. 'But what about the heist on Christmas Eve?'

Izzie was enraged. 'There's no way we can take part in that now. When Lord Featherlow finds out what we were up to today, he'll most likely have us followed. We have to keep squeaky clean for the foreseeable future.'

*

Rizor Rochester's heart sank when he received the text message from his accomplice:

I'M OUT. YOU'RE ON YOUR OWN.

His appetite had been stimulated much more this time than last; he was at the point of no return. This time he wasn't going to let a small fortune slip through his fingers. He sat with head in hands for almost a minute before he thought of the perfect solution.

*

It was dark before Annabelle and Amelie returned to Featherlow Manor. Annabelle was nervous; she decided to find Lord Featherlow before she bottled out of owning up to the drawing. Amelie wished her luck.

Winston was in the drawing room when Annabelle entered. She looked pale and troubled, and he jumped up to help her to a chair. 'What on earth has happened?'

Annabelle burst into tears. 'I lied to you. Your mother didn't do that drawing – I did. I only did it because I so wanted you to approve of Freddie and Amelie's relationship. I shouldn't have done it. I'm so sorry. I told Amelie about it today, and she said I had to own up to you straight away.'

Winston raised an eyebrow. 'Why did you tell Amelie about it today?'

'Because I needed her to let me buy her the dress from Cherry Conti's that I drew in the picture. She was having none of it, though. She tried it on and looked like a princess, but she wouldn't let me buy it for her. As if that wasn't bad enough, Lady Sophie Trumpton tried to get Amelie arrested by planting a diamond bracelet in her bag.'

Winston's eyes popped, and Annabelle waved a hand in the air. 'I snuffed that whole debacle out at the onset. I'm afraid I lied again, this time to two police officers. I said I'd filmed the whole charade on my phone and that Cherry Conti's would have CCTV images proving Amelie's innocence and Sophie's misdemeanour. Would you believe it that Izzie turned up too? She tried her best to drag Amelie into the gutter. I'm proud to say I saw both Trumpton sisters off with their tails between their legs.'

Winston's eyes twinkled. 'I'm sorry.'

'YOU'RE sorry? What are YOU sorry for?'

'For not listening to you. Amelie sounds like a decent girl.'

'Oh, she is! She was very concerned about me lying to you. She made me sort that out straight away.'

Lord Featherlow stepped forward to embrace his wife. 'Promise that you'll never lie to me again.'

Annabelle let out a huge sigh of relief. 'I promise.'

*

One of the police officers scratched his head, then tapped away on a keyboard at the station. He was right! He knew he'd seen that bracelet before; it had been stolen from a party in Kensington last week. One of the guests had been Lady Izzie Trumpton. What a stroke of luck; the police needed to pounce before those Trumpton girls tried to offload it elsewhere.

Thirty minutes later the officers were shown into the drawing room of the Trumpton's west London townhouse. Lady Sophie and Lady Izzie stood before them. The officer chose his words carefully: 'We have reason to believe the diamond bracelet in your possession is stolen property.'

Izzie nudged Sophie as she spoke. 'It's not! My sister's had that bracelet for years.'

The officer spoke again: 'Lady Izzie Trumpton I am arresting you on suspicion of theft. Lady Sophie Trumpton, you are also arrested for being in possession of stolen goods.'

*

In the office at Featherlow Forbes, Rizor waited for Grant to go to the drinks machine before he approached him. 'I have an offer you won't be able to resist.'

Grant glanced over his shoulder; there was no-one in earshot. 'What's that?'

'Lord Featherlow trusts you. You have access to his security codes and the vault at Featherlow Manor. If you give me the code to the vault, I'll arrange for it to be cleared out on Christmas Eve while the Featherlow Forbes Christmas Spectacular is taking place.'

'What's in it for me?'

'Once I'm far enough away with a new identity I'll send you ten thousand pounds. You can either stay on doing your pathetic little job or use the money to move on to better things. It's risk-free for you. No-one will suspect *you* of being a traitor.'

'But the contents of the vault are worth much more than that.'

'You can take it or leave it. Do we have a deal?'

Grant held out his hand to shake Rizor's. 'Deal.'

23

TO CATCH A THIEF

The following evening Lord Featherlow, Freddie, Fabio and Grant took in the magnificent view of London from Freddie's suite at The Fortescue Tower. Lord Featherlow sensed the tense atmosphere in the room. 'If this weren't so serious, it would be quite exciting. Are you sure we should carry on with this spoof until Christmas Eve? We've got Grant's recording of his conversation with Rizor; can't we have our dodgy Global Head of Sales arrested straight away?'

Fabio shook his head. 'We need to catch him red-handed. He could always say his conversation with Grant was a joke, and that he never intended to go through with it.'

Freddie agreed with his cousin. 'We need to devise a water-tight plan that will see Rizor Rochester behind bars. It's the second time he's tried to take us all for fools.'

Lord Featherlow glanced at Freddie and nodded towards Fabio, who was distracted by the complimentary sweets on a coffee table. Freddie winked at his father. 'If it's OK with you, Fabio, I'll take the lead on this one. I've got time on my hands until I take over from you in January.'

Fabio sucked on a sweet. 'Fine with me.'

Grant raised his arms in the air. 'Where do we start?'

Freddie sat at a desk and made notes. 'We need a base away from prying eyes. I'll give Grant access to this suite until further notice. I'm sorry, Grant, but you'll have to act normally during the day. Any meetings concerning this project will take place after office hours.'

Fabio unwrapped another sweet. 'We should make Grant centre of attention at the Spectacular. The leadership team will model one outfit each, but Grant should wear several and appear in different places: not just on the runway. That way, it won't look strange to Rizor that Grant has easy access to the vault. He can be the epitome of the "Featherlow Forbes Man" – a VIP with a millionaire's lifestyle.'

Freddie looked up from the desk. 'That's brilliant thinking, Fabio! That way the bodyguards we'll need to recruit won't look out of place.'

Lord Featherlow frowned. 'Bodyguards? Surely Rizor will smell a rat at the sight of them?'

Freddie continued to make notes. 'Not if Grant tells him they're fake.'

*

At the drinks machine the next morning, Grant pressed "record" on his phone before divulging the plans to Rizor. 'That's fantastic news! Those buffoons are certainly making my life easy. Do they know how stupid they'll look with a couple of spoof bodyguards roaming around the room? The customers will be in hysterics.' Rizor's shoulders shook in amusement. 'I take it you'll be there early to help them set things up?'

Grant nodded and kept his voice low. 'I'll be there the day before.'

Rizor glanced around the office; everyone was busy working away. He looked Grant up and down. Do you think you could do the heavy lifting? If so, I'll pay you five grand upfront. The fewer people involved with this, the better. If you can shift the gold bars the day before it will be less work on Christmas Eve.'

'But you're not due at Featherlow Manor until Christmas Eve.'

'I'll book a hotel nearby and tie-up with you when I

get there. You'll need to move the bars at some stage during the day into your car; then you can meet me at the hotel and transfer them into mine.'

*

The wine bar was losing out on business as Fabio, Grant and Fifi headed straight for the suite at The Fortescue Tower after work for the next three nights. Freddie and Amelie phoned through to the nightly meetings from Featherlow Manor. Grant's latest revelation caused a slight concern.

Fabio scratched his head. 'But there *are* no gold bars. What are we going to do? Could we fill some boxes with bricks?'

Freddie grimaced. 'Grant will need to meet Rizor the night before Christmas Eve and divulge there wasn't an opportunity to move the bars. He can advise that the heist should take place towards the end of the Christmas Spectacular after my jewellery collection has been launched. We'll make sure the schedule for the day frees up Grant for an hour so that Rizor is comfortable there's a timeslot for the robbery.'

Fifi cringed. 'I hope you guys know what you're doing.'

Amelie felt her friend's angst down the phone. 'It would be great if you could come to the manor the day before Christmas Eve too, Fifi. You can stay with me in the dower house.'

Fifi glanced at Grant. 'OK, I'd like that. I think Grant's going to need more protection than those bodyguards can offer.'

Amelie winked at Freddie and Fabio looked at his watch. 'Sorry, everyone. I've got a hot date tonight; I've put her off all week. I'll need to bow out now. Have a great weekend!'

The call ended, and Grant glanced sideways at Fifi. 'Freddie says the room service is excellent at The Fortescue Tower. He's encouraged me to make use of his account while we're working so late every night.'

Fifi blushed. 'I've always wanted to try lobster.'

Grant grinned. 'Would you like champagne with it?'

Fifi winked. 'I certainly would, Mr McGuire!'

24

BACK AT THE MANOR

On the 22nd of December, a delivery arrived at the manor for Lord Featherlow. He was pleased Annabelle had taken Amelie into town to have their hair done. That gave him the opportunity to open the Cherry Conti box and take out the dress. He was really out of his comfort zone this time. Giles knocked on his dressing room door and handed over the Dowager Lady Featherlow's diamond necklace and earrings. He saw the dress hanging from Lord Featherlow's wardrobe door and turned a bright shade of crimson.

Lord Featherlow didn't notice; he was too embarrassed about how he was going to divulge a strange set of events that had occurred since his mother had died. Giles left the room, and Winston opened a drawer in a walnut cabinet. He took out his mother's silver mirror and hairbrush. They were a gift from her parents on her eighteenth birthday. The brush contained strands of her white hair, and the mirror she had looked into every day of her adult life had gone cloudy.

Winston held the brush in his right hand and the mirror in his left. He looked into it. There she was again; he could just about make her out – she was smiling this time. Winston coughed. 'I take it you're happy I bought the dress. I do feel that you and Annabelle have ganged up on me ever since Freddie met Amelie. Well, you'll be delighted to hear you don't need to bother me anymore. I'll fall in line with your wishes – just stop spooking me out!'

With the brush and mirror back in the drawer, Winston sat down and held his head in his hands. How could he possibly get Amelie to wear the dress and the diamonds? His wife had failed with the dress, and Amelie refused to accept the diamonds from Freddie. There must be a way to keep the Dowager Lady Featherlow happy so that she stopped returning to haunt her son.

Giles knocked on the dressing room door. 'The ladies are back M'Lord.'

Winston shuddered. 'I'll meet Amelie in the drawing room. Please advise her.'

Amelie had just returned to the dower house when Giles turned up at the front door. 'Lord Featherlow would like you to meet him in the drawing room at the manor immediately. I drove round as the snow is slippery underfoot. I'll take you over there now.'

Amelie stepped into the drawing room, and Lord Featherlow signalled for her to sit down. 'I don't quite know how to say this without sounding like an old fool, but my mother won't leave me alone until you agree to marry Freddie.'

Amelie frowned. 'Are you saying your mother is still in touch with you?'

'She certainly is. She's not going to rest in peace until her beloved grandson is settled.'

Winston opened a drawer in a sideboard and pulled out a silver frame. 'I've even had to put her photograph away as I swear she's keeping an eye on me.' He handed the frame to Amelie who gasped in amazement.

'Your mother visited me at the Christmas Sparkle Ball, I'd recognise her anywhere.'

'Did she say anything?'

'Yes. She said something about being "acquainted with the Dowager Lady Featherlow" and that "she was a great woman". She also said it had been a pleasure to meet me and that "it'll soon be Christmas".'

'That sounds like my mother. Christmas it is then.'

'What do you mean?'

'She wants to rest in peace by Christmas. Also, Annabelle has her heart set on you becoming engaged to our son at Christmas. We need to make it happen – for my sanity if nothing else.'

Amelie lowered her eyes. 'But I didn't think I had your approval.'

Winston shuffled his feet. 'You made Annabelle stop lying to me. I'm forever in your debt.'

Amelie frowned. 'Freddie may not want to propose to me.'

Winston rubbed his hands together. 'He'll propose as soon as he sees you in that dress.'

'What dress?'

'The one you wouldn't let Annabelle buy for you. I've bought it instead. It would be rude to refuse a present from your future father-in-law.'

Amelie jumped up and hugged Lord Featherlow. 'I really hope you're right.'

Winston blushed. 'You have to wear my mother's diamonds with it. That should keep her quiet.'

'When should I wear it?'

'Christmas Eve. We wouldn't want to upset my mother now, would we?' Winston sighed. 'I couldn't possibly cope with that.'

Giles drove Amelie back to the dower house with a large garment bag, and red velvet box containing the diamonds, on the back seat. Her heart was bursting with excitement. Freddie had been in London for three days and was arriving back tomorrow with Grant and Fifi. All the plans were in place for the Christmas Spectacular and Amelie had never felt so happy in her life.

*

When Winston confided in Annabelle about buying the dress for Amelie, she was thrilled. 'I wanted you to be able to give your drawing to the happy couple. So, I had to get the dress right. What makes you think Freddie will propose on Christmas Eve?'

'Your mother had a vision – it's her prediction. She said it was to do with a flock of geese . . .'

Winston held his hands over his ears. 'I don't want to hear any more. My mother keeps popping up all over the place.'

Annabelle smiled. 'She will be so proud of you, Winston. All she ever wanted was to leave behind a happy family. We've had a blip, but now we're back on track.' Winston still had his ears covered, so Annabelle changed the subject. 'How are you getting on with your search for a yacht?'

Winston dropped his hands and bent down to pick up a glossy brochure from a pile under his desk. 'I've narrowed it down to three. Of course, you'll have the final say, my darling. Would you like a look now?'

Annabelle beamed. 'That would be wonderful. Let's sit by the fire in the drawing room. It's so pretty in there now in the evenings when the Christmas tree's lit up. There's such a good view from the window of the ones lining the drive. The guests on Christmas Eve are in for a treat!'

25

LAST NIGHT OF LUXURY

Fifi and Grant were spending their last night at The Fortescue Tower. Fifi ate a tempura battered prawn and smiled at Grant. 'I could get used to this.'

Grant pulled her close. 'We will be OK, won't we, once all this glitz and glamour has died down?'

Fifi rested her head on his shoulder. 'We were OK before, weren't we? If anything, I'll be pleased when we get back to normal. I'm not relishing the thought of you being protected by those bodyguards on Christmas Eve. How many are there going to be again?'

'Two. They'll not let me out of their sight.'

Fifi sighed. 'Well, I hope they don't take their eyes off the ball. You're far too important to me to get injured in a heist.' Fifi glanced sideways at Grant. 'It was very kind of Freddie to give up his suite for tonight and move into Amelie's apartment. Do you think he's trying to be a matchmaker?'

Grant blushed before checking his watch. 'I don't know what you mean. Why don't we go outside for some fresh air?'

Fifi pretended to shiver. 'I don't think so. It's freezing outside.' She reached for her glass of wine.

Grant stood up and held out his hand. 'Come along. You don't want to undo all that good work you did at Boot Camp, do you? A bit of exercise won't hurt. We only need to go out for an hour.'

Fifi swung her legs off the sofa. 'Oh, all right. If you insist.'

If there was one thing you could say about The Fortescue Tower, the lifts to the suites were always available and fast. Fifi felt like a celebrity when a butler pressed the button for their sixty-three-floor descent. The lift doors opened onto the hotel foyer, and Grant took hold of Fifi's hand. A uniformed chauffeur walked towards them. 'Your car awaits, Mr McGuire.'

Fifi's mouth fell open. What was Grant playing at?

A slow drive through the centre of London, in a limousine the week before Christmas, was an experience like no other. Fairy lights adorned the trees lining the Thames, and the London Eye was lit up brighter than ever before. There were glittering Christmas trees outside glitzy hotels, and partygoers oozed out of the open doors of heaving restaurants. Fifi was enjoying the show from the car window until it stopped outside the ice rink.

'Why have we stopped here?'

'We're going skating; we missed our session the other week.'

Fifi clung to the white leather seat in the back of the limo. 'I don't think so. I would have given it a go, but I've had two glasses of wine, and you wouldn't want me breaking my ankle so close to Christmas, would you?'

Grant chuckled. 'You're not getting away with it this time. I've booked the whole rink for an hour so that you won't be embarrassed when you fall over.'

'What do you mean "when" I fall over? I might be pretty good at this, Grant McGuire!'

'Come along then, let's go, the clock's ticking.'

Grant dragged Fifi out of the car and through the entrance to the rink. He put on a pair of ice skates, and Fifi sensed he was nervous. 'Go on then. You're the expert; show me your moves. I'll watch and learn for a while.'

Grant skated onto the ice, and Fifi felt a tap on her shoulder. She turned round to see Father Christmas on ice skates holding onto a sleigh. 'Your carriage awaits, my dear.'

Fifi burst into a fit of giggles. A skating elf appeared next; he whispered into a reluctant Fifi's ear. 'If you get into the sleigh you'll get a glass of champagne.'

Fifi climbed into the sleigh and Father Christmas and the elf pushed it to the centre of the rink before disappearing. Fifi couldn't see where Grant had gone. It was quiet on the ice; the only noise was coming from the distant revellers outside. Fifi sat with her hands in her lap, admiring the massive Christmas tree on the edge of the rink. The lights on the tree went out, and Fifi gasped. She felt another tap on her shoulder; this time it was Grant. He handed her a bottle of champagne and two glasses.

Fifi gulped. 'What are you playing at?'

Grant leant into the sleigh and kissed her on the lips. As soon as he did so, the tree lights burst into a colourful twinkling display and the sound system came to life with a rendition of "White Christmas". Fifi clutched onto the bottle and glasses and watched in awe as Grant skated around her; his backspins and Axel jumps timed to perfection.

When the music ended, Grant climbed into the sleigh. He reached into his pocket and produced a solitaire diamond ring. 'Will you marry me, Fifi?'

Fifi squealed. 'You bet I will!' She planted a kiss on Grant's lips and hugged him before staring at him in amazement. 'How on earth did you learn to skate like that?'

Grant shrugged. 'It was just one of my childhood hobbies. Shall we have some champagne?' Grant took hold of the bottle from Fifi and popped the cork. He poured it into the flutes before squeezing his fiancée. The music started up again, this time the song was: "It's the Most Wonderful Time of the Year".

Fifi rested her head on Grant's shoulder. 'How long do we get to sit in this sleigh?'

Grant checked his watch. 'Another thirty minutes.'

Fifi grinned, that left no time for her to do any skating. She held her hand in the air, and her diamond glittered under the artificial lights. She couldn't wait to show it to Amelie.

*

Freddie lay on Amelie's bed in her apartment. He thought back to the shy, awkward girl he had first met. Amelie had blossomed into the woman Freddie knew she could become. He opened a white leather box and took out a princess cut aquamarine and diamond ring. The colour matched Amelie's eyes to perfection. His grandmother's vision was about to come true. Freddie was going to propose to his princess in the snow on Christmas Eve.

26

ONE DAY TO GO

Fifi and Grant travelled from London to Featherlow Manor by train. Freddie joined them at the station. 'Well, well, well. I knew my suite at The Fortescue Tower would work wonders. Amelie's going to be thrilled when you tell her your news. Nice ring, Grant. Good taste.'

Fifi clung onto Grant's arm. 'Are you sure tomorrow's event is going to go without a hitch? I think you're all taking on a bit much with the customer event and a heist.'

Freddie sat forward in his seat and kept his voice low. 'The absurdity of it all is that there will be nothing in the vault. My father has cleared out the family jewels; there *are* no gold bars, and my jewellery collection is in here.' Freddie patted the case next to him.

Fifi raised her eyebrows. 'So, how are you going to catch a thief when there's nothing to steal? Won't Rizor turn nasty when he realises he's been tricked?'

Grant patted Fifi's hand. 'Our plan is foolproof. The event is going to be held in the ballroom. The bodyguards will wheel in Freddie's jewellery collection in a bulletproof glass cabinet after lunch. It will remain on display until they ceremoniously wheel it out at four o'clock. That's when Rizor will believe everything's in the vault and I'll lead him to it with the code.'

Freddie smiled. 'We've set up CCTV cameras so we can film Rizor entering the vault and rummaging around the empty boxes we've put in there. Grant will shut the door and lock him in.'

'It sounds dangerous to me.'

'Don't worry, the bodyguards won't let Grant out of their sight until the operation is over. We've hired the best of the best.'

*

Amelie had been invited to join Lord and Lady Featherlow for breakfast in the morning room of the manor. She glanced over at the make-shift desks that had been set up for her and Annabelle to use and felt disappointed that their whirlwind taste of Events Management was nearly over. Annabelle sensed Amelie was feeling melancholy. 'I've enjoyed our little dip into Events Management too. I have an idea.'

Winston raised an eyebrow and waited to hear his wife's latest plan. 'After Freddie and Amelie's wedding, we should open up the manor grounds to the public. We could also hold weddings and events in the ballroom. Amelie doesn't need to go back to work in the office; she can take over the role of Head of Operations here.'

Amelie blushed. 'Freddie hasn't proposed yet. It might never happen.'

Winston put his knife and fork down. 'Do you know what? I think that's a jolly good idea. We'll need someone we can trust at the manor when we're off on our yacht.'

Annabelle glanced at her husband before cutting into a slice of bacon. 'I don't want to be on a yacht the whole year-round. A few holidays will do me fine. Once the novelty's worn off, you'll realise that home is where the heart is.'

Winston pierced a sausage with his fork. 'If you want to be back here doing your little Events Management hobby, I may stay out at sea. I've always wanted to take up fishing.'

Annabelle smiled. 'What a great idea, Winston! It would be good to have separate hobbies. Too much of each other would be a bad thing.'

Amelie tried not to giggle as she spoke to Lord Featherlow. 'Did you know that Chad Lagerfield sails? You could have a chat with him tomorrow about it. I'm sure he'll be into fishing too. He's a real action man.'

Lord Featherlow's eyes twinkled. 'I've always rated Chad. He's a good guy. I might just take you up on your suggestion, Amelie.' Winston winked at Annabelle. 'Looks like you're going to be married to an action man.'

Annabelle choked on a grilled tomato. 'Who?! Chad Lagerfield??'

Winston sipped his coffee. 'No. Me!'

*

At eleven o'clock the doors to the morning room flew open, and Freddie strode through to embrace Amelie. Lord Featherlow was on a walk of the grounds, and Annabelle sat at her desk checking the last-minute details for tomorrow.

Freddie grinned. 'I've just had the best news on the journey down here. Come on in, you two.'

Fifi and Grant entered the room with Fifi waving her left hand around. 'Can you see it sparkle? It's the best ring ever – because Grant bought it. Freddie has been a real matchmaker; he even gave up his suite at The Fortescue Tower to get my fiancé to realise there's no better girl for him than me.'

Amelie dashed across the room to hug her friends. 'Your news has made my day! Do you know that Freddie noticed you two were crazy about one another before I did? His instinct is unbelievable.'

Annabelle smiled from her desk. 'Very many congratulations to both of you. I love a good romance. Why don't you young people go and celebrate? I can manage here. I think the least you men should do is take your ladies into the village for a slap-up lunch.'

Amelie smiled at Annabelle and mouthed the words: 'Thank you.'

Freddie walked over to kiss his mother on her cheek, and she held onto his arm. 'I need a very quick word with you if I may.'

Amelie had left the room with Fifi and Grant, giving Annabelle the chance to express her concern to her son. 'Fifi will need a ballgown for tomorrow. I'll be wearing one of my old ones, and your father has bought a new one for Amelie.'

Freddie's eyes were like saucers. 'Father has bought a dress for Amelie?'

'He certainly has. From Cherry Conti's, I might add.' Annabelle blushed. 'Amelie's won him over for some reason I can't quite put my finger on. I knew it wouldn't take long for him to see the goodness in her.'

Freddie felt a massive sense of relief. All he ever wanted was for Amelie to be accepted into the family fold. 'How can we get a dress for Fifi?'

'She'll suit fuchsia with that pretty blonde hair and blue eyes. Would you like me to order one for delivery first thing in the morning?'

'You're a star, Mother. We'll keep it a surprise until then. Fifi will be delighted.'

*

Archie's Alehouse was packed with revellers the lunchtime before Christmas Eve. Amelie and Fifi clung on to one another; they couldn't believe what had happened in just three months. Their lives had changed completely.

Fifi whispered to Amelie. 'This all began when Grant and I tried to stop your wedding to that hairless pumpkin.'

Amelie threw a hand to her mouth. 'I suppose that's a good description. I would have been marrying him tomorrow!'

Fifi glanced at her friend. 'You don't have any regrets do you?'

Amelie shook her head. 'Not at all; I'm in a daze.

My feet haven't touched the ground for the last three months. Fairy-tales don't come true, do they?'

Fifi smiled. 'Of course, they do. Look at Grant and me. I never thought Grant had it in him to buy me a whopper diamond ring and propose in the middle of an ice rink. My guess would have been a Haribo ring in the wine bar after work.'

Amelie giggled before closing her eyes and making a wish: If this was a fairy-tale she never wanted it to end.

*

Rizor Rochester was on the train. He hoped Grant would come up with the goods tonight. He'd already decided he would flee with the gold bars and avoid the embarrassment of strutting his stuff in front of Featherlow Forbes' major customers tomorrow.

*

Following a long and leisurely lunch, the foursome headed back to the dower house. They spent the walk home giving Grant tips on how to handle Rizor Rochester when he met with him at seven o'clock in a local hotel.

By six-thirty Grant was nervous. Freddie ordered a taxi. 'Here, knock this whisky back. Just go to the hotel, ask the taxi driver to wait for you, deliver the news to

Rizor that you didn't have chance to access the gold bars today, jump in the taxi and you'll be back with us within the hour.'

The whisky gave Grant some backbone. He strode into the hotel foyer to the sight of Rizor; and held his arms out to the sides. 'No luck today, it will all happen tomorrow.' Grant turned round and climbed back into the taxi.

Rizor clenched his fists then raised his eyebrows at the sight of the person walking towards him carrying two cocktails. Rizor took hold of one and took a big sip as the person spoke: 'You don't need to work with that bunch of losers. I know what they're planning. Work with me. Do we have a deal?'

Rizor held out his hand for his new accomplice to shake it. The cocktail tasted good. Rizor wasn't in the driving seat anymore. Surprisingly, he trusted the person who was.

27

THE CHRISTMAS SPECTACULAR

Fifi was summoned to the morning room by Lady Featherlow. Her mouth flew open at the sight of the fuchsia satin ballgown with lace overlay hanging from a curtain rail. 'What a beautiful dress! Will you be wearing that today?'

Annabelle smiled. 'No, *I* won't be wearing it. *You* will. Amelie and I will be wearing ballgowns, so I bought you this one as a little engagement present.'

Fifi caught her breath before bursting into tears; Annabelle handed her a handkerchief. Fifi blew her nose. 'You are sooooo kind! I feel like Cinderella.'

Annabelle placed an arm around Fifi's shoulders. 'The pleasure's all mine. I always wanted a daughter. Now that you and Amelie have entered my world, I feel like a new woman. I can't wait until we get dressed up. If you need to borrow any shoes, then I believe we're the same size.'

Fifi didn't care if it was the correct etiquette or not, she threw her arms around Lady Featherlow. 'Thank you so much. I'll never forget this. I feel like I'm in a dream.'

Annabelle chuckled. 'We'll all feel like we're in a dream with the Christmas Spectacular today. Let's go to my dressing room to choose you some shoes then Giles will drive you over to the dower house to get ready with Amelie. We need to be in the ballroom by eleven o'clock to greet our guests.'

*

Freddie and Grant entered the ballroom at ten-fifteen. They were both wearing Featherlow Forbes evening attire; Grant adjusted his bow-tie. 'What time are the bodyguards arriving?'

'Fabio's booked them to get here for ten-thirty. He says they've been fully briefed.'

The doors to the ballroom opened, and several members of the leadership team walked in. Chad Lagerfield was beaming. 'What time are we on the runway?'

Grant checked the schedule. 'Eleven-thirty. We'll need to wait in the drawing room while the customers are arriving. You look good, Chad, in our new Country Casuals range.'

Chad winked. 'I feel like the Lord of the manor.'

Fifi rushed into the room in her fuchsia ballgown. Grant couldn't believe his eyes. 'You look amazing. I'm the luckiest man alive to have you as my fiancée!'

Fifi curtseyed. 'Why, thank you, Mr McGuire.'

Freddie smiled. 'You look great, Fifi. Have you got him?' Fifi pulled Sparkles out of the folds of her skirt and handed him to Freddie. 'Brilliant! Thanks, Fifi, say nothing to Amelie.'

Fabio walked into the ballroom, followed by two bodyguards. He was wearing Featherlow Forbes' latest City Gent attire, along with a grin from ear-to-ear. He whispered to Freddie, 'It's great the guys turned up on time.'

Fifi clung onto Grant's arm before speaking in a low voice. 'Those men don't look very discreet. I'm surprised their holsters are on show. Shouldn't they be wearing jackets? They look more like weight lifters than bodyguards. They're more bulked up than Brendan.'

Amelie entered the ballroom in a cloud of turquoise chiffon, and Freddie's heart leapt. His grandmother's vision would become a reality later today. He glanced out of the window at the snow-covered grounds then turned his gaze to the magnificence of the tastefully decorated ballroom. The window sills overflowed with an array of holly and ivy foraged from the manor grounds the previous day. The runway for the fashion show was edged with planters of winter greenery, berries, and pinecones; and large vases of red roses were strategically placed to provide the most significant impact.

Freddie was mesmerised as he watched the fairy lights, adorning the trees both inside the ballroom and outside in the grounds, change from subtly glittering to shining brightly as the morning sky darkened from light grey to charcoal. There it was – he just knew it! It was snowing. There was only one person that could turn a grey day into a magical winter wonderland; the Dowager Lady Featherlow's timing was spot on.

Amelie touched Freddie's arm. 'What are you hiding behind your back?'

Freddie was brought back to the present. 'Nothing! I must round up the leadership team and hide them in the drawing room before the customers arrive.' Freddie bent forward and kissed Amelie on her cheek. His eyes glowed as he took in the full sight of her. 'I have never seen anyone look more beautiful. I can't wait for this event to be over so that I can spend time with you. I love you, Amelie Briggs.' Freddie kissed her again and then dashed off out of sight.

The bodyguards in their tight white shirts and skinny black trousers made their way to the drawing room too. Lord Featherlow frowned and turned to his wife. 'I don't know where Fabio got those gentlemen from, but won't they be cold? It's snowing outside. Should we lend them a couple of jackets?'

Annabelle shook her head and tutted at Winston's old-fashioned mentality. Fifi stood next to Amelie. 'Fabio was supposed to get proper bodyguards, not male models.'

Amelie chuckled. 'At least they've got guns.'

Fifi raised her eyes to the exquisite ballroom ceiling. 'Strapped to their muscly shoulders for everyone to see.'

Amelie smiled. 'That can't be a bad thing. Rizor won't try anything silly when he sees the guns.'

*

With the customers seated, the fashion show began. Grant was first on the runway with his bodyguards. There were gasps and claps from the audience. Chad Lagerfield was next, and he certainly knew how to strut his stuff.

Fabio appeared to cheers from the customers. He took his time on the runway with some breakdance moves before taking off his bowler hat and throwing it into the audience.

Annabelle clapped and whispered to Amelie. 'I'm quite enjoying this.'

Grant appeared again; this time he waved from the ballroom balcony. He was wearing a black fedora hat, black shirt, and cream linen suit. The bodyguards stood next to him flexing their muscles.

Fifi nudged Amelie. 'I didn't know Featherlow Forbes did a Gangster range.'

Amelie chuckled. 'I think Grant quite suits it!'

Rizor Rochester looked surprisingly at ease when it was his turn. He was wearing Featherlow Forbes' Uniform range. Rizor had chosen a pilot's outfit and saluted to the Head of an airline in the audience. He puffed out his chest; that had been a lucrative contract to win – Featherlow Forbes would miss their Global Head of Sales when he was gone.

Grant appeared several times more; down the aisle of the audience; on the balcony again; on the runway with the leadership team. The bodyguards never left his side.

Freddie was the last member of the leadership team to emerge; he'd coaxed Amelie into joining him, and they made a stunning couple in their evening attire as they glided down the runway arm in arm.

For the finale of the show, the leadership team lined the runway to rapturous applause before the sound system erupted with a rendition of "Simply the Best". All eyes turned to the slowly-opening doors of the ballroom to witness Grant walking through wearing a black leather jacket, jeans, white T-shirt, and trainers. The bodyguards appeared on either side of him in matching gun-wielding poses. The customers gave a standing ovation, their cheers and whistles bringing smiles to the faces of the leadership team. Fabio grabbed hold of Freddie. 'We did it! We pulled it off!'

Grant flashed a dimpled smile and Fifi went weak at the knees; trust Grant to make the simplest outfit of the day look like a million dollars. Lord Featherlow let out a sigh of relief. That was the easy part; he shuddered to think what the afternoon's events might bring.

28

THE JEWELLERY LAUNCH

The customers were ushered into the magnificent great hall for pre-lunch drinks, while the ballroom was transformed from a fashion show setting into a dining room. Lord Featherlow had contacts, and a local Michelin Star Chef had agreed to provide a food tasting session before taking time to mingle with the VIP guests.

Grant sidled over to Rizor. 'I'll meet you at the vault at four o'clock. Don't be late; we've only got a one-hour timeslot to shift the goods.'

Rizor nodded and turned round before smirking. Grant McGuire treated him like a fool. It was a good job his new accomplice had intercepted the plot to bring the great Rizor Rochester down and devised a new plan that would leave Featherlow Forbes well and truly out of pocket.

Annabelle checked her phone; she had seven missed calls from Cherry Conti. She went into the morning room to call her back. When Annabelle returned to the great hall, she was close to tears. Fifi noticed and linked her arm through Annabelle's before leading her outside onto the snow-covered steps of the manor.

'What on earth's happened, Lady Featherlow?'

'It's such dreadful news. Cherry has advised me that my payment for your dress has bounced. The payment for Amelie's dress the day before from Winston was approved. I have no idea what's going on. I'm highly embarrassed.'

Fifi turned the same shade of fuchsia as her dress. She needed to make sure she didn't spill anything on it over lunch as it would need to be returned. 'There must be a simple explanation, Lady Featherlow. Has your husband just bought his yacht? Maybe there's a delay in finances coming and going. I'm no expert in that field.'

Annabelle shook her head. 'Winston hasn't ordered the yacht yet.'

The Featherlow Forbes hand-bell rang, and the VIP customers made their way back to the ballroom. Annabelle was shaking, and Fifi held onto her arm. 'It's freezing out here. We need to concentrate on getting through today, and then we can find out what's happened with Cherry Conti's. It may even be a mistake at their end.'

Fifi was on red alert over lunch. Those bodyguards weren't doing their jobs properly; they were paying more attention to the female guests than Grant. Fifi was about to storm over to focus their minds back on their work when she heard whispered voices behind her. 'The money got transferred without a hitch. Just the jewels to go now.'

Fifi glanced over her shoulder. She could see Rizor, but not the person who had spoken to him. Just when things couldn't get worse, Fifi noticed one of the bodyguards had left his gun behind a vase of roses. How reckless was that! Fifi went over and picked it up. It was light; it was plastic, and it had a "Made in China" label on the side. Fifi was livid. The men were as fake as their guns! She grabbed Fabio and dragged him outside. 'Those men aren't real bodyguards, are they?'

Fabio frowned. 'As far as I know, they are.'

Fifi stamped her foot. 'What do you mean "as far as you know"? You were given a job to get the best of the best. Didn't you interview them?'

Fabio hung his head. 'I passed the task over to Chad. I thought he'd do a better job than me.'

Fifi held her head in her hands before realisation hit

her. 'How did you pay for the so-called bodyguards?'

'I gave Chad my uncle's credit card details. I couldn't afford to pay for two bodyguards in one go, not with Christmas around the corner. You have to admit that Chad came up with the goods.'

Fifi let out a strangled cry and Fabio raised his arms in the air. 'Is anything wrong?'

'You are in serious trouble, that's what's wrong! The bodyguards are fake, and Chad's cleared out Lord Featherlow's bank account.'

Fifi turned round and stormed back into the manor. Lunch was over, and the tables were being cleared in advance of the launch of Freddie's jewellery collection.

At two o'clock, the ballroom curtains were closed, and the lights turned out. Pulsating music emanated from the sound system, and the bulletproof glass cabinet was wheeled in by the bodyguards. Only Fifi was aware that one of them was minus a plastic gun. The lights turned on to rapturous applause.

Freddie stood next to the cabinet and presented his jewellery collection to the intrigued audience. Lord Featherlow had never been so proud. He wondered why his wife was snivelling at his side; he guessed she was proud too.

By three o'clock, it was time for the guests to

mingle; view the jewellery closer and collect Featherlow Forbes catalogues and gifts. The day was running to plan; the jewellery would be wheeled back to the vault at four o'clock.

Fifi had to think quick. She grabbed Grant and alerted him of her findings. 'So, you see, we're now in serious trouble. Due to Fabio's incompetence, Rizor and Chad have taken control. I bet the cabinet isn't even bulletproof. Who was supposed to organise that?'

Grant grimaced. 'Fabio.'

Fifi sighed. 'Well, Chad and Rizor now have access to Lord Featherlow's finances. My guess is they'll steal Freddie's jewellery and do a runner. It'll be you locked up in the vault while they make a quick getaway.'

'How are we going to turn this around?'

Fifi's eyes blazed. 'I need a gun. A real gun – just make sure it's not loaded. You have twenty minutes to get me one. I'll meet you by the vault.'

Grant went in search of Giles. 'This will sound very strange, but we need a gun for the finale of our event today. Can you please take one out of Lord Featherlow's gun cabinet and make sure it's not loaded. We're only using it for demonstration purposes.'

Grant met Fifi at the vault and presented her with a rifle. 'Great! I'll hide under the stairs, and you turn up as planned to meet Rizor. There are ten minutes to go.'

At four o'clock the bodyguards wheeled the cabinet to the enclave surrounding the vault. They high-fived each other, and one of them announced: 'That's us done. It's easy money when you can get it.'

Fifi raised her eyes and kept as quiet as a mouse. Grant walked into the enclave and waited by the vault door. Rizor entered next. 'Well, are you going to open the vault for me?' Grant opened the vault, and Rizor shoved him inside before closing the door.

A man in a balaclava was next on the scene. He smashed through the glass with a hammer and shoved the jewellery into a suitcase. He signalled to Rizor to join him outside. Rizor glanced over his shoulder then followed. The suitcase was thrown onto the back seat of the waiting vehicle whose driver was wearing a Joker face mask. Rizor was surprised there was another accomplice; he thought the proceeds of the heist were going to be split between him and Chad. He jumped into the front seat and the man with the hammer climbed into the back.

Fifi dashed out from under the stairs and positioned herself in front of the getaway vehicle. 'STOP RIGHT THERE – OR I'LL SHOOT!'

The Joker removed his mask and Fifi took a step back at the sight of Lord Featherlow. Freddie removed his balaclava and Rizor reached for the door handle to make a run for it. Lord Featherlow had already pressed the central locking button. He wound down his window.

'Excellent work, Fifi. The police are on their way. Fabio advised me of his conversation with you. It caused me great concern, so Freddie and I decided to take action. I left it to Fabio to deal with Chad Lagerfield. He's now been handcuffed and locked in the drawing room with Fabio on guard. I knew those handcuffs my nephew bought me for Christmas a few years back would come in useful for something; he also bought me the Joker mask. He's a laugh a minute that boy.'

Two police cars sped down the drive, and four officers jumped out. Lord Featherlow poked his head out of the car window. 'You've been fully briefed. There's just one robber to be arrested in here and another in the drawing room. Now that we can leave things in your capable hands, we need to return to our guests.'

29

FREE AT LAST

The exit of the Featherlow Forbes leadership team and VIP customers couldn't come quick enough. The Christmas Spectacular event had gone so well that several of them wanted to linger around for a chat. It was six o'clock before Lord and Lady Featherlow had their home back to normal. They liked it best when just the family were around. Fabio said his goodbyes and Grant and Fifi were about to leave to catch the last train to London.

Annabelle stopped them. 'It would give Lord Featherlow and me the greatest pleasure to offer you accommodation at the manor tonight. It's far too risky to get the train back to London in the snow. It's falling thick and fast.'

Grant glanced at Fifi. 'Well, it's been quite a day. It would be good to take time to reflect on the past twenty-four hours. If Lord Featherlow is in agreement, then we should accept.'

Fifi squeezed Grant in delight, and Lord Featherlow nodded his agreement before pouring Grant a whisky from a decanter. Annabelle whispered to Fifi. 'You won't have too much time to reflect. Freddie's going to secure the deal tonight. We'll be having a party!'

Fifi widened her eyes. 'Freddie's going to propose to Amelie tonight?!'

Annabelle crossed her fingers. 'I sincerely hope so, or Winston's mother will haunt him to his dying day.'

*

In the dower house, Freddie had blindfolded Amelie. 'Just let me lead you. Stop arguing.'

'Where are you taking me? I've had enough suspense and mystery for one day.'

Freddie untied the blindfold, and Amelie felt the heat of the roaring fire as he positioned her in front of it. Two stockings were hanging from the mantelpiece. She gasped when she saw a mince pie, carrot, and glass of whisky next to the fireplace.

Freddie held a finger to his lips and turned her round to look out of the window. Snow was falling, and at first, she couldn't see what she was supposed to be looking for. Then, in the shelter of the branches of a magnificent Christmas tree, she saw Sparkles.

Amelie held her hands to her mouth. 'I know there are so many Christmas trees about, but that one wasn't there yesterday, was it? Who put it there, who decorated it?'

Freddie took Amelie's hand and led her outside. 'You need to retrieve Sparkles quickly, or he'll become sodden in the snow along with the both of us.'

Amelie reached into the tree to rescue Sparkles. Freddie got down on one knee in the snow-covered grass. 'Will you marry me, Amelie? You have been destined to be the next Lady Featherlow since the day I was born, my grandmother predicted it.'

Amelie laughed as flakes of snow landed on her eyelashes. 'You'll need to show me the ring first.'

Freddie grinned. 'I'll let Sparkles do that.'

Amelie studied the polar bear and noticed a ring attached to its diamante collar. She unfastened the collar, and the ring slid into her hand. Freddie took hold of it. 'Will this ring do? It matches your eyes.'

Freddie slipped the ring onto Amelie's finger, and she twirled around in delight. Freddie stood up and brushed the snow off his trousers. 'Is that a "yes".'

Amelie hugged him. 'It's a definite "yes", Freddie Featherlow. What took you so long?'

*

Back at the manor, Annabelle took the photograph of the Dowager Lady Featherlow out of the drawer. 'It's rude of you, Winston, to keep your mother incarcerated like this. She should be on display on the sideboard.'

Fifi and Grant chuckled as Lord Featherlow raised his eyes. He gave Grant a yacht brochure to look at while he ventured up to his dressing room. Winston hesitated as he opened the drawer of the walnut cabinet. He took out his mother's silver brush and mirror. He looked into the mirror, which was no longer cloudy. It was as clear as the day it had been given to her on her eighteenth birthday.

Winston waited for five minutes then put the brush and mirror back in the drawer before returning to the drawing room. He rang the bell for Giles. 'Please bring up our finest champagne from the cellar. We have something to celebrate.'

Annabelle did a little clap in delight and winked at Fifi. Grant sipped his whisky and felt honoured to be associated with this eccentric family.

Giles brought the champagne in on a tray and smiled at Lord and Lady Featherlow. 'Master Freddie and Miss Amelie are walking up the drive.'

Everyone went to look out of the window. Freddie

and Amelie were walking hand-in-hand through the snow. Amelie carried Sparkles under her arm, and before they climbed the stone steps to the manor, they kissed.

Lord Featherlow glanced over at the silver photo frame with the picture of his mother. The black and white photograph didn't look quite so menacing. He could even make out a hint of a smile on the Dowager Lady Featherlow's lips. Winston felt a weight lifting from his shoulders. With no-one looking, he picked up the frame, kissed the glass, and whispered, 'All is well, Mother. You can rest in peace now.'

The floodlights outside the manor shone down on Amelie, accentuating her necklace and earrings. Freddie's eyes glistened. His grandmother would be delighted Amelie was now the proud owner of her diamonds.

Fifi poked her head out of the front door. 'Come on in, you two. You must be freezing. I can't wait any longer – I need to see your ring.' Freddie saw Grant waving through the window, along with his parents who raised their champagne flutes in the air.

Amelie giggled. 'What are you two still doing here?'

Fifi shrugged her shoulders. 'We're far too important to Featherlow Forbes to make that long journey home in such heavy snow. Freddie's parents insisted we stay at the manor tonight.'

Amelie ran up the steps, and Fifi grabbed her hand. 'It's beautiful! It matches your eyes. Aren't we just the luckiest girls? We won't forget this Christmas for the rest of our lives.'

When he reached the top of the steps, Freddie turned round and looked to the sky. The snow-filled clouds parted briefly to the sight of a shooting star. Winston saw the star from the window too. He punched the air – his mother was finally gone. He was free!

Annabelle stood next to her husband. 'What little game are you playing at now?'

'I don't play games, my darling.'

'Why is there a star on top of the dower house?'

Winston held his head in his hands. 'She'll never leave me; she's got stuck!'

Amelie stepped outside to find Freddie. 'What are you still doing out here?'

Freddie placed an arm around Amelie's shoulders and nodded towards the dower house. 'Father Christmas is bound to find us tonight.' Amelie gasped at the sight of a massive star attached to a chimney. 'I had the star erected at the same time as the tree.'

Amelie kissed her fiancé. 'You are so thoughtful. Thank you for turning my world upside down.'

Freddie grinned. 'This is just the beginning, Amelie. We have a blank canvas, and I intend to paint it in the brightest colours possible. You trust me to do that, don't you?'

Amelie giggled. 'I do, Freddie Featherlow. I do!'

****

Printed in Great Britain
by Amazon

41473163R00118